C0-BWX-407

SNOWBOUND WITH THE SINGLE MOM

AMY RUTTAN

H Harlequin

MEDICAL ROMANCE

If you purchased this book without a cover you should be aware that this book is stolen property. It was reported as "unsold and destroyed" to the publisher, and neither the author nor the publisher has received any payment for this "stripped book."

H Harlequin®
MEDICAL ROMANCE

ISBN-13: 978-1-335-99340-3

Snowbound with the Single Mom

Copyright © 2025 by Amy Ruttan

All rights reserved. No part of this book may be used or reproduced in any manner whatsoever without written permission.

Without limiting the exclusive rights of any author, contributor or the publisher of this publication, any unauthorized use of this publication to train generative artificial intelligence (AI) technologies is expressly prohibited. Harlequin also exercises their rights under Article 4(3) of the Digital Single Market Directive 2019/790 and expressly reserves this publication from the text and data mining exception.

This is a work of fiction. Names, characters, places and incidents are either the product of the author's imagination or are used fictitiously. Any resemblance to actual persons, living or dead, businesses, companies, events or locales is entirely coincidental.

For questions and comments about the quality of this book, please contact us at CustomerService@Harlequin.com.

TM and ® are trademarks of Harlequin Enterprises ULC.

Harlequin Enterprises ULC
22 Adelaide St. West, 41st Floor
Toronto, Ontario M5H 4E3, Canada
www.Harlequin.com

HarperCollins Publishers
Macken House, 39/40 Mayor Street Upper,
Dublin 1, D01 C9W8, Ireland
www.HarperCollins.com

Printed in U.S.A.

Recycling programs
for this product may
not exist in your area.

Ares cursed under his breath as the wind howled down, whipping up the snow. "I will admit it's hard to come from the tropics to... to this."

"You're regretting your decision, aren't you?" Pauly teased.

"No. I'm looking forward to the mountains and the work. Also spending time with my godson. And you."

Pauly's heart fluttered and she couldn't help but smile up at him. It was the way he said you, so softly and so tenderly. As their gazes locked, his dark eyes were twinkling at her and a strange feeling went through her.

You're just lonely. Lonely and tired. It's nothing.

Pauly tore her gaze away and tucked an errant strand of hair behind her ear.

He was her friend, her best friend. There was no way she was going to even entertain the idea of something more than that.

One, Ares loved his lifestyle. Two, he'd sworn off settling down years ago. And three, there was no way she was going to ruin what she had with him.

She wasn't going to lose his friendship.

Dear Reader,

Thank you for picking up a copy of Pauly and Ares's story, *Snowbound with the Single Mom*.

I love being able to set books in my beautiful country of Canada, especially setting it in a place I've been. Canmore is a special town in the mountains near Banff and it was so much fun to set a story here.

Pauly is a warm, loving mom who is navigating life after the loss of her husband. She's a pretty amazing supermom, but even supermoms get lonely.

Ares has been Pauly's best friend forever. He was her and her late husband's roomie in college, he's her son's godfather and he's always been head over heels in love with her.

Now he's in Canmore to help her and his godson out. As they grow closer, he wonders if maybe he'll have a chance with the woman he's always loved.

I hope you enjoy Pauly and Ares's story!

I love hearing from readers, so please drop by my website, www.amyruttan.com.

With warmest wishes,

Amy Ruttan

Born and raised just outside Toronto, Ontario, **Amy Ruttan** fled the big city to settle down with the country boy of her dreams. After the birth of her second child, Amy was lucky enough to realize her lifelong dream of becoming a romance author. When she's not furiously typing away at her computer, she's mom to three wonderful children, who use her as a personal taxi and chef.

Books by Amy Ruttan

Harlequin Medical Romance

Caribbean Island Hospital

Reunited with Her Surgeon Boss
A Ring for His Pregnant Midwife

Portland Midwives

The Doctor She Should Resist

Falling for the Billionaire Doc
Falling for His Runaway Nurse
Paramedic's One-Night Baby Bombshell
Winning the Neonatal Doc's Heart
Nurse's Pregnancy Surprise
Reunited with Her Off-Limits Surgeon
Tempted by the Single Dad Next Door
Rebel Doctor's Boston Reunion

Visit the Author Profile page
at Harlequin.com for more titles.

This book is for all single parents out there
and especially the ones I know who are
doing an amazing job.

**Praise for
Amy Ruttan**

"*Baby Bombshell for the Doctor Prince* is an emotional
swoon-worthy romance.... Author Amy Ruttan
beautifully brought these two characters together
making them move towards their happy ever after.
Highly recommended for all readers of romance."
—*Goodreads*

CHAPTER ONE

PAULY GLANCED AT the arrival board at the Calgary International Airport.

Oh good. I'm not late.

Or at least she wasn't late to pick up Ares. Objectively, she was running behind and had been worried—what with the hour and twenty-minute drive from her place in Canmore to Calgary, on Halloween, with the first significant snowfall happening the night before, *plus* her son, Jeremy, being a-stick-in-the-mud about wearing his snow gear to school and almost missing his bus—that she was going to leave poor Ares standing out in the cold.

Literally.

It was one of the coldest and snowiest Halloweens she could ever remember since moving to Alberta, so *of course* it was the day she had to go to the airport. She didn't usually like to leave Jeremy alone. No, he wasn't alone, he was at school. But she never went this far from town without him.

She was trying hard not to think about it too

much and instead focus on how excited he'd be when he came home and saw his godfather.

She also hated running late, which was just adding a whole other level of stress.

Thankfully, the fates were in her favor, and Ares's flight from Toronto to Calgary had been delayed. She just hoped Ares was ready for snow, because she knew for a fact that Toronto was a lot warmer than Alberta at the moment.

Also, he had been traveling all over the world as a locum paramedic and first responder and his last job had been in the Caribbean, so she knew it was going to be a shock to his system. Pauly had only been in Canmore for three years and she still wasn't used to the dry cold of southern Alberta.

There were times, especially in the dead of winter, that she missed the milder climes of southern Ontario. She was sure Ontarians would disagree that it was more temperate there, but it was true. Still, she wouldn't trade her life here to move back. She loved being in Alberta and in the mountains, particularly.

Her late husband, Rex, had always dreamed about becoming a paramedic and first responder who worked in the mountains. He'd loved climbing. Pauly had too, once. That had been before she had Jeremy. Once she'd become a mom, she couldn't put her life on the line to scale mountains for fun. Rex had always loved the thrill far more than she did. She was glad, though, that they'd been able to make Rex's dream come true and move out here.

Only, it had been short-lived. Nearly two years ago, an accident had claimed Rex while he was at work on the mountain, leaving her and their then eight-year-old son all alone.

For the last two years Pauly been numb.

There had been moments she agonized over it, worried that maybe she could've protected Rex. Which was ridiculous. He'd died doing his job. Still, it ate away at her.

Family had come and helped her on and off over the last couple of years as she'd tentatively gotten back to work, but now she was facing the reality of maybe moving up from the desk job she'd taken at the paramedic station, and actually getting back out there in the field.

Part of her wanted it, badly. She was a field paramedic. The problem was Jeremy. There was a niggly little piece of her brain that was terrified of the idea that something could happen to her, and she'd leave Jeremy an orphan.

She wasn't sure how this was all going to work.

Since Rex had died, she'd made sure Jeremy had all the love and support he would've gotten had his dad still been there. She and Rex had always managed to balance everything. Now there was no time for anything else—her life revolved around her son.

Lately though, it felt like she was failing there too, and that scared her.

She didn't want Jeremy to ever be lonely, to feel the lack of a parent's attention. That was a feeling she knew all too well, and she swore she'd never put her kids through that. But the truth was, Jeremy was craving a father figure. It made Pauly feel so guilty that no matter what she did, she couldn't seem to fill that void for him.

So when, on one of their frequent virtual calls, Ares had said he was taking a sabbatical from his usual firm, and had offered to come and help her out, it had felt like a life line.

"You don't have to do that. I'll be fine."

She hoped that her voice didn't crack, because the truth was, she wasn't fine. She hadn't been fine since the accident. And she most definitely wasn't fine since all her extended family had returned back to their lives, leaving her and Jeremy alone.

Ares made a face. "You're lying to me."

Pauly chuckled. "How do you always know?"

He grinned, those dark eyes twinkling. "I think you said the same thing to me years ago, when I stopped going to classes after my parents' divorce. You called me out then and now I'm doing the same."

Pauly took a deep breath and relaxed. "I hate that you know me so well."

Ares shrugged. "That's what friends are for."

"You have a life to lead."

"So do you," he said, firmly. "Pauly, I love you and Jeremy. Let me come and help you out. My contract will be through in five days. I have to head back to Toronto and put in for my sabbatical, which I'm due, and then I can work and help you get back on your feet in Canmore. You know I love the mountains out there. Let me do this for you. Let me do this for Rex."

Pauly choked back tears. "I'm so glad to have you as a friend."

"Of course."

"And the guest room is open for you. I don't want to hear about you getting your own place in Canmore. Besides, it's a bit harder to come by accommodations when ski season starts."

"After all these years, I better be able to crash at your place," he teased. "Try not to worry. I'll see you in a week."

It had been the longest week of Pauly's life. Especially since Jeremy had found out that his godfather—or "Uncle Ari," as he liked to call him—would be coming to stay with them for the next year. There was an actual smile on Jeremy's face, real joy in his life, just at the thought. It had been so hard to find that little inkling of happiness since his father died.

When he'd gotten on the bus this morning, with his Halloween costume firmly packed in his rucksack, he'd been going over all the big plans to go trick-or-treating with Uncle Ari.

Ares has no idea what he's gotten himself into.

Just that thought brought a smile to Pauly's face and eased the anxiety she'd been feeling. She didn't want to rely on anyone, but she really could use Ares's help. Between her job and Jeremy, there was so much to juggle.

It was terrifying doing it all on her own. Lately, she felt like that lonely little girl she'd once been, left alone while her parents worked double shifts. The one who had spent her childhood raising herself and her little brother.

You're not alone anymore though.

There was a lot of chatter and the arrival doors opened up.

Pauly looked up to see a stream of people coming out the doors. She easily spotted Ares in the crowd. It was hard not to pick him out. A six-foot-three bronzed Greek god striding through the airport with a huge duffel bag slung over his shoulder. His dark brown hair was longer than she remembered, a bit flyaway. His skin was a deeper tan from the sun of the tropics. It really did look like he'd stepped off the beach. He was athletic and moved through the crowds quickly.

When his gaze landed on her, she waved frantically, smiling, and he grinned back.

When they were at college, every single girl she knew was in love with Ares Galanis. She may have been with Rex, but she could definitely see the appeal.

He opened his arms as he approached, dropping his huge duffel bag. "Pauly!"

"So glad to see you," she said, trying to hold back the rush of emotion she was feeling in that moment as his arms came around her and she snuggled against him for one of his warm hugs.

The last time she'd seen him in person had been at Rex's funeral. She didn't really remember that. Everything about that horrible day was a blur, but she had snippets of memories, of seeing Ares in her periphery taking care of Jeremy.

He had always been there for them, and she was glad he was here now. For the first time in a long time, she felt a bit of relief, some comfort and safety.

Instantly, the guilt hit her for feeling that with someone other than Rex, because Rex had been the first. The first to take care of her and comfort her.

Truly.

Ares has always made you feel that too.

Pauly stiffened and stepped out of Ares's embrace, wrapping her arms around her core to steady herself, otherwise she was going to get overly emotional and start blubbering.

One thing she'd learned as a child relying on herself—keep your emotions in check.

"You're a big girl." Her mother's words echoed in her head. Always the same reminder, when-

ever she broke down while her parents worked overtime.

She shook those horrible memories away.

"How are you feeling?" Ares asked.

"Today? Frazzled. I was worried I was going to miss your plane. I know you probably don't appreciate it, but I was very thankful for your flight delay."

Ares shrugged. "Flight delays are the norm in my line of work."

She glanced around him. "All you have is a duffel bag?"

"It's a large duffel. It's what hockey players use."

She cocked an eyebrow, fighting the smile that was tugging at the corner of her lips. "You can fit your whole life in there?"

He glanced down at the duffel. "Yes. This bag goes with me everywhere. Do you have a problem with it?"

"No. It just seems...you travel light."

"Well, I did ship out my rock climbing stuff. I didn't want to carry it on the plane, and I don't exactly trust airlines not to lose my luggage. So that will be coming in the next couple of days."

The moment he said the words "rock climbing stuff" she tried not to visibly wince. "That makes sense."

"I'm a nomad. I don't need much. This bag is my best friend." He winked, teasingly, knowing that she considered herself the deserving owner of that title.

"I hope you have winter gear in there," Pauly mused.

Ares frowned. "What? No."

"You climb mountains and you don't have winter gear?"

"It's bulky, so I shipped that too," he explained. "It's October. I didn't think I'd need it right away."

"Oh, you're in for a shock, my friend. We'll get you to a shop and get you some warmer gear. You'll need it for tonight."

Ares picked up his duffel as they headed out of the arrivals area and toward the parking garage where her truck was parked. "Tonight?" he asked, querulously.

"Trick-or-treating. Jeremy has elected you as his official trick-or-treat partner. He even has a rubber mask you can wear."

Ares rolled his eyes, but he was smiling. "I forgot today was Halloween."

"It's hard to forget when you have a kid."

A strange brief look fluttered on his face, which gave her pause, but only for a second.

"Well, yes. I suppose I don't really track the holidays much. The kiddie holidays, that is."

"Kiddie holidays?"

Ares grinned. "Carnival in Rio is something to experience."

"Oh, I'm sure." Pauly was a bit envious of his

freedom. She'd gotten married straight out of college. She and Rex had immediately put down roots and made a life together.

As Ares had stated, he was a nomad. A traveler. Never staying still.

They stepped outside and he cursed under his breath as the wind howled down between the airport and the parking garage, whipping up the light dusting of the first snow. "You have snow?"

"It snowed in Ontario during some Halloweens."

Ares made a face. "I will admit it's hard to come from the tropics of my last job to...to this."

"You're regretting your decision, aren't you?" she teased.

"No. I'm looking forward to the mountains and the work. Also spending time with my godson. And you."

Her heart fluttered and she couldn't help but smile up at him. It was the way he said *you*, so softly and so tenderly. As their gazes locked, his dark eyes were twinkling at her and a strange feeling went through her.

You're just lonely. Lonely and tired. It's nothing.

Pauly tore her gaze away and tucked an errant strand of hair behind her ear. "Come on, we better get you some warmer clothes and then get back to Canmore before Jeremy gets home."

She was glad that Ares was here, but the other things she was feeling about him were strange. He was her friend, her best friend. It had only been two years since she lost Rex.

The only way she could rationalize it was that she had missed the intimacy, the companionship. But there was no way she was going to even entertain the idea of something more than that with Ares.

One, he loved his lifestyle. Two, he'd sworn off settling down years ago. Pauly knew that for a fact; she'd been there when that commitment was made. And three, there was no way she was going to ruin what she had with him.

She wasn't going to lose his friendship.

She's your friend and nothing more.

Ares had to keep reminding himself of that. It was clear from their previous calls and video chats that Pauly was struggling. Not that he blamed her in the least. His heart was still hurting after Rex's death. He couldn't even begin to imagine what Pauly and Jeremy were going through. Although Pauly would never admit it.

She was strong, something he'd always admired about her. While he and Rex were usually goofing off during college, she'd been looking after them. Making sure they ate right, attended classes. Pauly had always been responsible.

All he could offer her during that time immediately after Rex's death had been a shoulder to cry on. For the last two years, she had a lot of family helping her out, but now that was gone. Ares knew her family and Rex's had begged her to move back to Ontario, but Pauly had made it clear she loved it in Canmore, so did Jeremy. They had scattered Rex's remains amongst the Three Sisters and she had stated, in no uncertain terms to everyone, she wasn't dragging Jeremy away.

Ares was glad to be able to take this year, take a position in Canmore and try to help her as much as he could as she made this transition back. It was the least he could do. But he had to keep reminding himself that she was *just* a friend.

Of course, he'd been doing that since the day they met.

Her heart had always belonged to Rex, and Ares cared for Rex too.

Both Pauly and Rex had been there for him, supported him in times his family hadn't. They had been there in college when his whole world had fallen apart. When his parents, who he thought were the epitome of love and longevity in marriage, split.

And it had not been amicable.

Part of Ares blamed himself, because he and his father had had a blow-up argument six months before his parents' marriage ended. He hadn't even been on speaking terms with many of his family. But the final split had made Ares rethink his whole ideal of love and marriage.

Most importantly trust.

As the years went on, both his brothers' marriages had failed too, and his sister's was perpetually rocky. It was clear to Ares that marriage just didn't work.

It worked for Pauly and Rex.

Except "worked" was hard to quantify, in that case. Rex had died. If he hadn't, maybe even he and Pauly would've eventually split.

Ares hated the negative thoughts filling his mind. He pushed them away. Rex and Pauly had been his best friends. When he'd seen her at the funeral, she'd been hollow, a shell, and he knew her heart was shattered. As much as he wanted to be there for her, she had her family around her, so he'd kept his distance. Now was his chance, finally, to help her out.

Honestly, when he'd gotten off the plane in Calgary, he'd been pretty sure that this year would be easy. That he'd gotten over his tender, unwelcome romantic feelings about Pauly. And then he'd seen her standing in the arrivals area.

It was like she hadn't changed at all. She was the woman he remembered from college.

Her dark brown hair was longer than before, swept back in a side bun. Her long dark lashes hid stunning clear blue-gray eyes and her luscious red lips parted in a smile that completely lit up the room. The moment Ares saw her, his heart sped up with anticipation and he realized right then and there he'd been a fool to think he'd moved on.

He'd been in love with her for far too long.

It was bad enough that he was in love with someone he couldn't have, that no one he'd met since had held a candle to her. But, to top it all off, he wasn't even *looking* for someone to settle down with—ever.

He'd already irrevocably disappointed his parents when he hadn't followed in his father's business footsteps, so there was no point in trying to please them by marrying. It hadn't worked for them, and it probably wouldn't for him.

At least, that's what he kept telling himself. Because deep down there was a part of him that kind of envied what Rex and Pauly had had.

Now, as they traveled to a shop to buy him some better winter gear, Ares couldn't help but feel this sense of happiness to be with Pauly again. A joy that was conflicting with his own grief over the loss of Rex.

At least Pauly looked a bit better now. When they'd scattered Rex's ashes, she'd been lost. Pale, and just broken. Nothing like her usual self.

He wondered if she even really remembered him being at the funeral.

"Here we are," Pauly announced as she parked her big white truck in the parking lot of an oversized big-box outdoor supply store. She was smirking at him. "I still can't believe you packed so light for winter in Alberta."

"I've been spoiled in the tropical countries," he said.

"You really have," she teased.

They climbed out of the truck and hurried inside the store. There was a single second when he did regret his decision to come, with the cold biting at his skin. But it was only for a moment.

It's the jet lag. That's why I wasn't thinking straight about the weather. That's all any of this is.

Pauly would probably tease him about this for some time. Even though she was the responsible roommate, she'd always poked fun at the pair of them. That was okay. Ares liked their jokes, their ribbing. It had been a long time since she'd ragged on him. A little bit of the old Pauly was shining through.

The store was, thankfully, warm and it didn't take them very long to find Ares a thicker coat, a hat, gloves and boots. Once that was all purchased, they grabbed a quick bite to eat and got back out on the Trans-Canada Highway to head to Canmore.

The service for Rex and the spreading of his ashes had been in the summer, when they'd all been able to take the trail to the meadow, filled with wildflowers, which overlooked the mountains.

There were definitely no wildflowers out in the fields as they drove west now. There was snow, blowing snow, lots of it, and when they came to sections of the highway that were just open fields, the whiteness really did blind them.

It reminded Ares why he hated winter—why he always spent these months somewhere warmer.

"You're scowling," Pauly said, breaking the silence.

"Am I?"

"One thousand percent."

"Winter," he grunted.

She giggled softly. "I did warn you."

"I hope this subsides before tonight," he groused.

Pauly snort-laughed in that adorable way she always did. "Well, you won't get so much drifting in town, but it'll be cold."

"Great."

Pauly glanced at him briefly and they shared a smile. He loved seeing her smile again, but he could still see that sadness, that hesitation in her blue-gray eyes.

"Jeremy is going to be so excited to see you," she remarked, interrupting his thoughts.

"I'm excited to see him too." He loved his godson; he could endure winter for Jeremy. "What's he going to dress up as?"

"I can't tell you. He wants you to be surprised."

"Should I be worried?"

She grinned. "No, but I swore no hints."

"Fair enough."

He settled back to enjoy the drive into the mountains as they chatted about nothing in particular. It was just easy to talk to her—it always had been. Ares couldn't wait to spend some time climbing these peaks, all the ones he used to climb with Pauly and Rex a long time ago. It was just the cold bothering him. He'd have to build up an immunity to it again.

The mountains were hidden by clouds of flurries, but then they rose out of the clouds of snow, like great Goliaths of rock.

He was envious of Pauly being settled here, of getting to see this every day.

I could settle here myself.

He quickly ignored that little thought.

His life was too up in the air, too transient. He loved his work, and this placement wasn't permanent. He was only on a year sabbatical from his current job. There was an end date to his time here in Alberta.

Nothing could make him stay here permanently.

Really. Nothing?

CHAPTER TWO

PAULY WAS STILL inwardly chuckling that Ares had arrived in Alberta with no real winter wear. He was Canadian—he should know how the weather could be. But then again, he'd traveled so much the last fifteen years or so, that maybe he really had forgotten.

That was the way he always had been, ever since they were in college together. Always a little bit disorganized. When she, Rex and Ares had all shared an apartment together in Toronto, Ares's bedroom had generally been a catastrophe. So even though they weren't those carefree college kids anymore, it kind of made Pauly happy to know that not much had changed about him. Something was still the same in her life.

The drive back to Canmore was peaceful. They chatted about the flight and a bit about Ares's job in the Caribbean. Pauly was just forever grateful that he was willing to put his life on hold for this year while she properly got back to work and regained her footing after her world had been shattered.

Her world, and Jeremy's.

There were still times when Jeremy wasn't okay with Pauly leaving his sight, and she hated that for him. She hated that her child was feeling so anxious that he couldn't be a kid right now, that he felt like he had to protect his mom. All Pauly wanted for Jeremy was for him to enjoy his childhood and not worry about her, or anybody.

She didn't want Jeremy to go through what she had.

"Mommy," Pauly said over the phone. "When will you be home? It's dark and Sam is crying."

"You're a big girl of ten, Pauly. Keep the lights on and stay with Sam. You're his big sister and he needs you. Daddy and I both have to work late."

"Okay." She held back a sniffle.

"No crying, Pauly. Just take care of Sam. You're in charge."

She realized now that she shouldn't have been in charge at ten years old. Jeremy was ten and he needed her still. Just like she'd needed her parents.

Which made her transition back to work all the more difficult.

It was the reason why she'd been stuck at the station or in town for the past year, rather than out on the trails. Jeremy struggled with letting her go back out on the mountain, especially near the trail where Rex was killed. And as much as she liked being in the field, it didn't bother her to keep closer to town.

Eventually, though, it would mean a demotion and she didn't want that. She was a paramedic. Highly trained. She wasn't meant to sit behind a desk, even if it was the safest place.

Sometimes we have to do things, sacrifice things we love, to keep others safe.

She swallowed the lump in her throat as she turned off the Trans-Canada Highway and took the roundabout that whizzed them in the direction of Canmore. Her three-bedroom townhouse was on Benchlands Trail, a little bit away from the picturesque and touristy mountain downtown of Canmore. She was closer to the crowded bike trails, but it was so worth it because her back porch gave her an unobstructed view of the Three Sisters.

"This is perfect," Rex exclaimed enthusiastically as he walked around on the deck.

"Sh... Remember, we don't want to be too excited. We want to make a decent offer," Pauly teased.

Rex grinned and pulled her close. "I can't help it. This is like a dream. Jeremy will love it here when we move next month."

"I think so too." She drank in the mountain air. "It is beautiful."

"This will be our home. You and me. Forever."

"You okay?" Ares asked, interrupting her thoughts.

"What?" Pauly asked, hoping her voice didn't shake.

"You just zoned out there."

She could see the concern etched into his face. Ares knew her so well. "I'm fine. Really."

"Hmm. I'm not buying that."

"I figured you wouldn't," she mused, as she signaled and then pulled into the driveway of her wooden-sided townhouse. "Welcome to your new home for the next year."

"I appreciate you letting me crash at your place, but I really can get my own place in town if it it's too much hassle for you," Ares offered.

"No. No way am I having my bestie renting an overpriced apartment. It's winter, ski season is gearing up, so everything else is gearing up too, like prices for hotels, restaurants, short-term rentals…"

He smiled. "Well, I'm looking forward to helping you out and working here."

"Me too."

It was nice to have someone else around. Another adult.

Don't rely on him though. This is all short term. You're on your own.

They climbed out of her truck, and she unlocked the front door. They had about thirty minutes to get Ares settled before Jeremy's bus dropped him off and then Ares would be bombarded.

"The guest suite on the lower level is yours. You know your way around."

Ares nodded and made his way over to the large bedroom on the ground floor of the townhouse, just off the entranceway and the door to the garage. When he came to visit them, this was always where he stayed, except during Rex's funeral, when the house had been full of extended relatives, like Pauly's parents and Rex's family.

Pauly trailed after him.

"This is perfect, Pauly. Really." He set his duffel bag on the floor.

"Would you like a coffee? Or I can let you get sorted. I have to start dinner and get some stuff set up for trick-or-treaters."

"I can help." There was a twinkle in his eyes as he peeled off his coat and set it on the bed. "It's been forever since I participated in Halloween."

"Okay, but first I'll make you a coffee, so you can enjoy that while I roast a bunch of pumpkin seeds."

Ares made a face. "Yuck."

"What?" she asked, laughing as she left his room and climbed the stairs onto the main level of her house.

"I've never understood that," he stated. "Roasting pumpkin seeds. I hate them."

"Oh, come on, you've never tasted my pumpkin

seeds. I season them with garlic and some with smoked paprika. I even do a maple sugar version."

"I just hate the outer shell. I think it's a sensory thing."

"So the world traveler is picky, eh?" she teased as they meandered into the kitchen.

Ares was grinning as he took a seat at the island. "I've tried my fair share of delicacies abroad and I'm not saying no to pumpkin seeds because I think they sound gross. I'm stating an actual fact—that I detest them."

"Well, I can't argue with that." Pauly turned on her coffee maker and then pulled out the pans she needed to lay out the seeds. "What's the weirdest cuisine you've tried on your travels? Like something you would've never eaten or even thought of eating before?"

"Probably a scorpion in Asia."

Now it was her turn to gag. "Bugs?"

"They're high in protein," he countered. "And sometimes, you're out in the wilds on a rescue mission or learning survival skills, and you have to eat bugs. Or prairie oysters."

"I've had those before."

He raised his eyebrows. "What?"

"I live in the west. Everyone has had them. Alberta has the best beef." She poured him a cup of coffee. "So you're telling me a bug is more desirable than a pumpkin seed?"

"Yes."

"You state that so firmly."

"Of course I do, because I'm completely right."

"I'm not buying it."

He grinned. "Well, the only way you could compare it is to eat a bug. A scorpion in fact."

She shuddered. "Well, you can't find that at the local co-op, so I'm going to say nope on that."

"Then concede I'm right. It's quite easy to admit it." There was a twinkle in his eyes and a smirk on his handsome face.

"You're still absolutely hopeless." She shook her head and handed him his cup. As he reached out to take the mug from her, his fingers brushed hers and she felt this rush flow through her, sending a ripple of heat through her blood.

It completely caught her off guard. She almost dropped the mug, so shocked by that flood of sensation just from a simple touch. She wanted to pull away quickly, but she didn't want to burn Ares's fingers.

And there was a part of her that liked it. It felt intimate and she'd missed that. Like she'd missed the connection. The laughter.

Sure, she had family around on and off, but this one-on-one with Ares was different to in-laws and parents and siblings.

Then she reminded herself that Ares was her friend. And he was a risk-taker, to boot. There was no way she could fall for a friend, especially one who took risks like Rex had.

As soon as Ares had a firm grasp of the mug, she pulled back her hand quickly and ran it nervously over her thigh, like she was trying to rub off the feeling of his warm skin.

She shouldn't like the fact that she had touched another man. It was wrong.

No. It's not. It's okay.

She ignored that small voice. It was the same one that had been telling her lately that it might be okay to move on, that Rex would want her to be happy, but it was hard to believe it. What she'd had with Rex felt like a fairy tale. No one was lucky enough in life to have that twice, and she wasn't going to take the risk on dating again, looking for it, not when she had Jeremy to worry about.

Ares didn't seem to notice anything as he put a little shot of hazelnut flavoring into his coffee. He was completely oblivious, and she was relieved about that.

"Bugs truly aren't bad," he continued, interrupting her chain of thoughts and easing her nervous tension.

"Really?" she asked, hoping her voice didn't shake. "I find that hard to believe."

"No, they're good."

"Well, don't pay me back by roasting me some," she teased as she pulled out the various seasonings she needed for the pumpkin seeds. "Although, I wouldn't mind some of your mother's spanakopita."

When they'd all been rooming together, they'd shared cooking duties, but Ares was absolutely useless in the kitchen. Except for breakfast, he was good at that. Thankfully, his mother would often send him food and her Greek traditional dishes were some of Pauly's favorites.

"Oh, I'm sure she'll ship you a batch," Ares remarked. "She always did like you and Rex."

"That would be nice."

What Ares wanted to say was how much his mother liked *Pauly*.

"You need to find yourself a girl like Pauly and settle down."

It was the constant rhetoric that his mother nagged him with. That and the fact that his parents really didn't think he'd grown up all that much, because he hadn't done the right thing and settled down and had children.

Like they had? he scoffed under his breath.

They were so worried about him and his life, when they should've been working harder on their own, and with their relationships with their kids.

Especially his dad.

His father had been so disappointed that Ares hadn't gone into the family business and taken over the restaurant. His father had never really seemed proud of what he did. He just didn't seem to get that Ares loved saving lives.

"What about Nico and Stathis?" Ares argued.

"What about them?" his father asked.

"They can take over the restaurant."

"Nico is on his way to be a surgeon and Stathis just got called to the bar. Now, if you wanted to go to medical school... I can understand that."

"A paramedic is just as important as a doctor," Ares snapped.

"But not as important as the restaurant. As the legacy. You're the youngest, Ares. You have to take it over before it dies. If you don't, then we're done."

"Then I guess we're done. I guess it dies."

Ares hadn't talked to his father much after that. And then his parents' marriage ended and everything just fell apart.

Honestly, he did sometimes think about becoming a doctor like his brother Nico, but he liked the freedom of being a paramedic. Then there was the cost of getting any more qualifications.

After turning down his dad's legacy, Ares had kind of been on his own.

The only one who never nagged him about his choices and just listened to him had been Pauly.

It had always been Pauly, his go-to for everything. But pursuing that connection was out of the question. Pauly had belonged to Rex and vice versa. Ares would never have gotten in the way of their love, because if he had, he would've lost them both.

It had been hard watching them. He was happy

for them, but he also longed for something that deep too.

"So, when I ask her to marry me you take the picture," Rex instructed.

"What if she says no?" Ares teased. *Although, a secret part of him kind of wished for that out-come...*

He instantly felt guilty, especially when Rex froze. "You think she might?"

Ares clapped his friend on the shoulder, hating himself. "No, man. She's going to say yes."

He had no doubt about that. Pauly and Rex loved each other. Rex was the luckiest man alive and Ares envied them.

Now, even though Rex was gone, he just couldn't do anything to risk his friendship with Pauly. She was too important to him.

There was a slam of the front door and Pauly smiled.

"We're in the kitchen, Jere!" she called out.

Ares set down his coffee and stood up as his godson came bounding up the stairs to the main level. When he was last here for Rex's memorial, Jeremy had clung to him. He'd been a rock to the young boy who had just lost his father.

And Ares was glad to do it. He was the godfather, after all, and that was something his family had always taken seriously. Even with all their issues.

Jeremy's face lit up at the sight of him. It made

Ares's heart ache. He saw Rex there in that ginger hair and the smattering of freckles on Jeremy's nose, but the eyes were all Pauly.

"Uncle Ari! You came!" Jeremy shouted, dropping his backpack on the floor and running at him at full speed.

Ares laughed and knelt down to catch the boy in his arms, holding him close. "Did you think I wouldn't?"

Jeremy stepped back. "No. I guess I didn't. You always keep your word."

"Of course." He tousled Jeremy's hair. "You've grown."

"He definitely has. I had to buy him new winter boots," Pauly remarked, setting a pan of pumpkin seeds in the oven.

"You're going to go trick-or-treating with me tonight, right?" Jeremey asked.

"Yes. I was told you had a secret costume and a mask for me."

"More of a hat. I'll go get it!" Jeremy raced off up the stairs to where his bedroom was, but not before stopping and leaning over the rail on the upstairs landing. "Mom, can we have pizza tonight?"

"Sure, buddy," Pauly said. "I'll order it now."

"Awesome!" Jeremy disappeared again.

Ares chuckled to himself. He'd missed Jeremy and Pauly. And he still missed Rex—always would. But he was glad he could be here for his wife and son. Even though they weren't blood, they were family all the same and Ares wanted to keep them safe.

"I think you'll get a kick out of his costume."

He turned to glance at Pauly who was holding back laughter and suddenly he was suspicious. "What is it?"

"I told you before, I am sworn to secrecy." She giggled again. "I need to order the pizza from the local place before it gets too busy."

"You're purposefully evading me."

There was a gleam in her eye. "I am."

Jeremy came rushing down the stairs in the getup of a vintage video game character, with the fake moustache and everything. "See!"

"Oh, so I'm going to be your brother?" Ares asked.

"No way." Jeremy pulled out a dinosaur hat, and suddenly Ares knew that he was going as the little green dragon this character often rode. It was a ridiculous hat, with big googly eyes on the top and Pauly was already laughing quietly behind him.

It was absurd.

Ares took the hat from Jeremy and strapped it on. It was heavy and hot and he turned to look at Pauly, who was doubled over laughing behind the counter.

"It's perfect!" Jeremy announced. "Hey, can I hop on your back and you carry me around?"

"No. I love you, buddy, but no." That was where Ares drew the line.

Jeremy chuckled. "It was worth a try."

"Jeremy, go grab that big candy bowl out of the storage room while I go pick up the pizza," Pauly said.

"Okay, Mom."

Pauly continued giggling as she passed Ares. All he could do was cross his arms and glare at her.

"I feel like I was set up." He knew the crazy big eyes on top of his head were moving around, because he could feel them shaking.

"It's so funny."

He huffed and rolled his eyes, but was only teasing. He really didn't mind doing this for Jeremy. It was one night, and it was obviously bringing him joy.

Pauly came up to him. "You look adorable."

His heart skipped a beat as he looked down at her, her long thick lashes brushing the top of her white cheeks, her lips so close. He was fighting the urge to wrap his arms around her and kiss her on the tip of her nose.

He had to get control of himself.

She wasn't his.

She was just a friend.

"Thanks," he replied, gruffly.

"I'll be back in a few minutes. Keep an eye on the pumpkin seeds, they'll be done soon."

"Maybe I'll let them burn in revenge for making me dress up so ridiculous," he groused.

She laughed. "I guess that's fair."

"Go get the pizza."

She waved over her shoulder and headed down the stairs. Ares took a deep breath and wandered over to the living room with the vaulted ceiling and big picturesque window. The snow was dissipating and the sun was starting to get lower in the sky, but he could see the Three Sisters in the distance. The sun was causing the snow caps to glow, almost pink, and he couldn't help but smile.

He'd thought he could handle this year, helping out Pauly and Jeremy. He'd thought he'd buried those feelings he felt for her deep down. But just a couple of hours with her, and everything he thought he had locked tightly away was bubbling to the surface.

Part of him wanted to run away, to run from those feelings, because it would be easier. He'd been doing that for a long time, but he wasn't going to leave Pauly and Jeremy. Not when he'd made the promise.

He had to stick out the year, even though it was going to be the hardest year of his life.

CHAPTER THREE

PAULY COULD NOT stop chuckling every time she pictured Ares in that ridiculous hat that Jeremy made him wear. It was so endearing, because Ares did it solely to make Jeremy happy. Ares was never one to dress up and make a fool of himself. Not even at all the college parties they attended.

Sometimes, in big crowds, he was a little bit more reserved. Whereas Rex had always been the life of the party. She sometimes wondered how the three of them had become so close. Whatever the reason, she was glad Ares was here now, taking Jeremy out trick-or-treating.

It was something Jeremy and his father had done every year. The fact that Ares was willing to do it now meant the world to her.

Jeremy's first Halloween without Rex had been so heartbreaking and hard.

This helped to make up for all of that.

Ares may have looked ridiculous in that green dinosaur hat, but he was also so damn cute. And

Pauly actually found it quite sexy, only because he was being such a good sport about it.

She paused, instantly feeling bad for thinking of Ares like that. To think of anyone like that. It was too soon.

I'm really hard up, she mused to herself as she finished off her glass of wine. She did miss physical touch and intimacy, but now was not the time and place to be dwelling on it. She'd had all that with Rex and now he was gone. Ares was just a friend with his own life to lead. If she ever did think about being with someone again, she needed someone grounded—not a self-proclaimed nomad.

There was a knock, and she headed to the door as she heard little voices on the other side calling out "Trick or treat!" She greeted the kids and parents, gave them their chocolate treats, then saw a very tired, tall dinosaur and her plumber son come walking up the driveway.

She laughed quietly behind her hand. It was too adorable.

"Hi, Mom!" Jeremy called out as he raced inside, leaving Ares behind. "We got a lot."

"Did you?" Pauly asked, smiling gently as Ares came in, shut the door, and took off the hat. His shoulder-length hair was a mess. Without thinking, she reached out and tenderly brushed some of it back.

Ares's gaze locked on her and her heart skipped a beat as she stared into his mesmerizing dark eyes.

What am I doing?

She pulled her hand away quickly. "Sorry."

"For what?" he asked, softly.

"For making you wear that ridiculous hat." It was a lie, but she didn't want to make things any more awkward and she certainly didn't want to chase him away by being all weird and clingy.

"Oh." He ran his hand through his hair. "It's fine. It was for Jeremy."

There was a knock at the door and she answered it.

"Trick or treat!" the little princess on the doorstep shouted.

"Why, Melissa, you look so cute!" Pauly gave her some candy, then looked up to greet Melissa's mom, Stacey, who was standing beside her daughter. She looked terribly pale. Instantly, Pauly had a feeling something was not right. "Stacey, you okay? You need to come in for a moment?"

"No...we're almost done," Stacey said, but it was breathy, like she was struggling for air. "I'm fine."

"I don't think you are," Ares said, from behind Pauly, and gently stepped past her, outside. "I'm Ares Galanis. Friend of Pauly and also a paramedic. You look exhausted."

Stacey looked him up and down, and wobbled a bit. "Maybe...maybe you're right."

"Come on, Melissa," Pauly said, holding out her hand to the girl. "Come see Jeremy. He'll put on some cartoons while we get your mom some water, okay?"

She tried not to show it, but panic was rising in her.

The last thing Melissa needed to see was her mom collapse. And Pauly could see all the signs of that happening soon—the gray pallor, the fine sheen of sweat, the way Stacey's eyes couldn't quite focus, making her appear a bit off balance.

"Okay, Mrs. Charpentier," Melissa said, taking Pauly's hand.

Pauly ushered her inside, and sent her bounding up the stairs to see Jeremy. Meanwhile, Ares helped Stacey in and escorted her to the small sitting room just off the ground-floor bedroom. Guests used it while staying, and sometimes Jeremy would come down and play video games there.

Ares got Stacey settled in a chair and helped her off with her coat while Pauly headed up to the kitchen to get a glass of water and an ice pack from the freezer.

When she came back down, Stacey had fainted and was now flat on the floor. Ares was gently calling to her and checking her pulse.

"What happened?" Pauly asked, kneeling down

next to her neighbor. "How long has she been out?"

"I saw her fainting and I knew she would hurt herself if I didn't get her to the floor. She's been out for a minute. Her pulse is weak, but she's breathing. I've called an ambulance. Do you know if she has any medical conditions?"

"She's diabetic," Pauly stated. "She looked like she was going to faint."

"That might explain it. Still, she needs to get checked out at the hospital."

Stacey roused. "What...why?"

"It's okay, Stacey," Pauly said, gently placing the cool ice pack on her neck.

Ares pulled out a pack of candy Rockets from his pocket—little pressed discs of sugared candy. They were gross, as far as Pauly was concerned, but they were a great thing for a diabetic who might be having a bout of hypoglycemia. It was that or orange juice, and Pauly didn't have any of that in the house.

"Stacey, take some of this candy and that should help." Ares unwrapped it for her and handed it over. He was so gentle and kind with his patients, something that Pauly had always noticed when they worked together in the past. It was part of why she'd recommended him for the open position at the station. She knew Ares would be a good fit for the team.

"Thanks. What happened again?" Stacey asked, confused.

"You fainted. Melissa is safe. Do you want me to call your husband?" Pauly asked.

Stacey nodded and Pauly went to call her husband, Ryan. She was anxious to let him know what had happened to his wife and daughter, and to reassure him that Stacey was safe and would be okay, that the paramedics were on their way. It was a reassurance she hadn't gotten when Rex was first reported missing.

Ryan said he'd be right over. By the time that call was made, the paramedics had arrived. Thankfully most of the trick-or-treaters in the neighborhood were done for the night, and the roads had been clear. There wasn't a lot of time for chitchat as Pauly directed her teammates on where to find Stacey. She could hear Ares helping them to get her on the backboard, telling them information about when she passed out.

Ryan arrived, looking pale. Pauly called for Melissa, and her dad gathered her up into his arms.

"Is Mommy going to be okay?" Melissa asked Pauly.

Pauly's feet felt like lead as she walked stiffly from the viewing room where she'd identified Rex. Her brother, Sam, was with her, saying things to her, but she couldn't hear him. All she could think about in that moment was having to

*break the news to Jeremy and tell him that Daddy
wasn't coming home.*

*When she got to the waiting room Jeremy was
curled up in a chair next to her mother-in-law,
whose face looked haggard. Pauly fought back
the tears that she wanted to shed, all the screams
and cursing she wanted to let out.*

She'd just become a widow.

"Mommy?" Jeremy asked.

*Pauly knelt down and wrapped him up in her
arms. "I'm here. You're not alone."*

*"Is Daddy going to be okay?" Jeremy asked,
in a small voice.*

"Of course," Pauly replied, swallowing her
emotions down, pushing away the memory. "You
know she's a diabetic, right?"

Melissa nodded. "Yep."

"It's most likely her blood sugar got a little too
low, but a doctor is going to check her out just to
be on the safe side," Pauly explained.

Melissa nodded.

"Thanks for helping," Ryan said. "It's good to
have paramedic neighbors."

Pauly smiled warmly. "Yes. It is a perk."

Ryan followed the stretcher out and all Pauly
could do was stand back and watch as they loaded
Stacey into the back of the ambulance. Ares was
standing next to her.

She was still lost in her own thoughts. All those
memories haunting her.

"They seem like good guys," Ares said.

"Who?" Pauly asked, absently trying to center herself.

Ares quirked his brow. "The paramedic team."

"Oh. Yes."

"You okay?"

"Fine."

"Pauly…"

"You'll be working with them tomorrow," Pauly interrupted him to try and stop the barrage of questions, because she didn't want to talk about this now. She plastered on a brave face as the ambulance finished loading and slowly made its way down her street. Big fat flakes of snow began to fall and the street was silent. Halloween was over.

They headed back inside. Pauly shut the door, taking a deep breath. Suddenly, she was just overwhelmed and exhausted.

"You really seemed out of it," Ares stated.

"Every year I think Halloween will be easy, but every year it's just a bit chaotic." She smiled, but it was forced. "What did you think of trick-or-treating?"

She knew she was changing the subject, and she didn't care. She didn't want to talk about her feelings right now and she was surprised how tonight was stirring up all these emotions she thought she had carefully locked away.

"Well, besides the strange looks I got that centered around the weird dinosaur hat and probably the fact I'm a face they haven't seen before, sur- prisingly good."

She breathed a sighed a relief inwardly that Ares hadn't continued to press her on the matter. It was another good thing about him—he knew when not to pry and poke.

"Good thing you had that candy in your pocket," Paul remarked as they headed back up the stairs.

"It was my payment," Ares said. "From my godson. I'm worth one whole Rockets roll."

She chuckled. "That's a pretty sad fee for wear- ing that hat."

"I agree. I hate Rockets."

She laughed. "Me too. It's pure sugar."

"I can't even get a chocolate bar?" Ares grinned. "Oh well, I'm glad he had fun tonight. That's all that matters."

And she appreciated that about him. Ares was so easygoing—he just went with the flow. "How about a glass of wine and some bad Halloween specials?"

"That's a deal. But I do want to head to bed early tonight. I want to be my best when I'm for- mally introduced to my new colleagues tomorrow. I hear that the person in charge of training me the first week is brutal. Kind of a control freak."

"What?" Pauly shrieked, giving Ares a playful punch on the arm as he laughed. "Ha. Ha. Very amusing."

"I thought so."

Jeremy had dumped all his candy on the counter for Pauly to check through, but he was munching on a mini bag of potato chips and watching one of the old classic Halloween cartoons she used to watch when she was a kid. Her nerves might be a bit frazzled, but at least her son was happy this year, and safe. They all were and Stacey would be fine.

Pauly pulled out a bottle of red wine, poured her and Ares a glass and headed over to the couch to join Jeremy. Ares sat down next to Jeremy, who covered him with his fleece blanket. Pauly curled up at the other end of the couch.

She tried to focus on the television, but she couldn't help but watch Jeremy and Ares together. It hurt her heart a bit. This time last year had been hard. It had been the first Halloween without Rex. Jeremy hadn't wanted to do any of the old things and Pauly hadn't pushed him.

How could she?

All she'd been able to think about was the year before that, when they'd been whole as a family. There'd been laughter, candy, badly acted spooky movies. Then, when Jeremy went to bed, she and Rex had talked about trying to have another baby.

There'd been so much hope in that conversation. She'd been excited about the future, even if it meant going through the in vitro fertilization procedure again—she'd such a hard time conceiving Jeremy. They had decided to try, because it would be worth it. They wanted to bring another life into the world and just expand their love.

But then, three weeks later, Rex had been killed in that accident. And then there was no more thought to that.

She'd been so hopeful about the prospect of another baby, but instead she was left broken and grieving.

All she had was Jeremy and she was fine with that, but still tonight brought up a lot of memories, of the plans that were snatched away from her. She was overcome with emotion. She was so glad Ares was here and seeing him with Jeremy just warmed her heart completely.

This was the Jeremy she remembered. The laughter—that was the sound that had been missing in her house. It was all so natural and so right.

It made her melt and for the first time in a long time, it felt like she and Jeremy were a little bit more whole.

Ares finished his glass of wine around the time that Pauly and Jeremy were headed off to bed. He was more than ready for sleep, because it was already close to midnight in Eastern Standard Time and he was having a bit of jet lag.

He thought it would be simple to fall asleep and be ready for his first day of work the next day, but he was completely wrong.

He tossed and turned, a million thoughts racing through his mind. Mostly, they centred around Pauly. That moment she had looked up at him when he'd been wearing the silly mask, the way their fingers had brushed each other... And there'd been a few times he'd caught her looking at him, which had absolutely taken his breath away.

Tonight on the couch watching old cartoon Halloween specials, it had felt cozy and right, even if it was snowing outside in October. For the first time, in a long time, Ares had felt completely comfortable and at home.

It had been a long time since he had that. Not since he was a kid. Back when his parents had been happy and Ares believed in the perfect family, believed that he had one. But no one was perfect.

It reminded him not to get *too* comfortable.

This was a bad idea.

It was too tempting.

Finally, he'd had enough fretting, and wandered upstairs to make himself some warm milk with some cinnamon in it. It was something his *yiayia* had always done for him when he struggled to go to sleep on Christmas, when his excitement overtook him and he knew his parents just wanted him to go to bed.

Although right now, he could go for a shot of his parents' secret stash of ouzo too, but he doubted that Pauly had a bottle of that tucked away.

He grabbed a mug and poured himself a glass of milk, microwaving it. He found the cinnamon and then glared at the container of spiced roasted pumpkin seeds on the counter. He carefully picked one up to try it.

The seasoning was good, but, yeah, he still didn't like the texture at all. It was nasty. Still, he choked it down, because he couldn't find a paper towel to spit it out in.

"So?" Pauly asked, coming down the stairs bundled up in an oversized fuzzy bathrobe. It made her look so tiny. Her dark hair was braided and hung over her shoulder. "I saw you try one."

"You scared me half to death," he grumbled, pulling out his warmed cup of milk.

"You scared me! I was wondering who was lurking down here, took me a moment to realize it was you."

"I couldn't sleep."

"I thought you would be out like a light, what with the time change and all."

Ares shrugged. "This happens a lot. I get over-tired and then I can't sleep."

"I should've told Jeremy you were too tired to take him out tonight."

"No," Ares said, quickly. "I was glad to do that with him. It made him happy."

Pauly smiled. "It did. Thank you. Last Halloween Rex's parents were here and we tried to get him to trick-or-treat, but he was so sullen, so not himself. It was good to see him smile with you. I appreciate it so much."

"He's my godson. I told you, we take that seriously in my family." Ares sprinkled some cinnamon in his warm milk.

"Warm milk?" Pauly asked, curious.

"Want some?"

She nodded. "Never thought of putting cinnamon in it."

"Something my grandmother would always do," he said, pouring another mug of milk and microwaving it. "Of course, when she made it, it was goat's milk and not two percent. So it was always so thick."

"Sorry, no goat's milk. I could put it on the grocery list."

Ares laughed softly. "Uh, no, that's okay. I'm fine with bovine dairy products."

"Are you worried about tomorrow?"

"No. Should I be?" He set the mug down in front of her. As he began to sip his own, he watched Pauly wrap her hands around the mug. Her delicate, soft hands.

"No. I was only teasing before. I think it will go smoothly. You're experienced, it's all just standard."

"I get it. Bureaucracy and all that."

"You've got it." She took a sip and made a *mmm* noise. When she set down her mug, there was a slight foamy moustache on the top of her lip. "So good."

He smiled at her. "You have a little something."

"What?" She stuck out her tongue, trying to lick it away, but she kept missing.

"No. Here let me." He gently touched her face, then ran his thumb across her lip. It was so soft and it made his blood hitch to touch her silken skin. Their gazes locked and his pulse thundered between his ears as he held her chin, staring at her.

What are you doing?

"Well…" He cleared his throat as he pulled away. "I think I should try and get some sleep. It'll be a long day tomorrow."

"Right. Yes." Pink tinged Pauly's cheeks. She set her empty mug on the counter by the sink. "Good night, Ares."

"Good night, Pauly."

He watched her scurry away, kicking himself inwardly for letting it slip again. For letting his emotions and feelings about her get the better of him.

He had to do better. She wasn't his and never would be.

CHAPTER FOUR

THE ALARM STARTED blasting music and Pauly bolted upright. She let the music play as the local news and weather reports started, but she was really only half listening to the reports that there was going to be snow and a low of minus twenty Celsius.

Typical.

She couldn't remember the last time she had slept so soundly. Well, it was probably two years ago, when Rex had been alive. Now sleep, if she did have it, was normally punctuated by many bouts of waking up, sometimes reaching out to see if Rex was there, though that hadn't happened in a while.

Her mind was usually a whirl of trying to keep track of everything so that nothing fell through the cracks, so she didn't make a mistake or miss something. So having a night where she didn't toss and turn was heaven. Apparently she'd needed it.

She had no clue that the simplicity of Ares's warm milk and cinnamon would do the trick. Or maybe it was the fact that there was someone else in the house.

Except, there had always been someone around, on and off.

She hadn't been left alone much. So what made Ares's presence so different?

She didn't know and she didn't have much time to sit there and ponder over it. Today was Ares's first day at the station. As soon as Jeremy got off to school, she was going to introduce Ares to the rest of the team and get him set up with a partner. Then she'd go through all the proper training modules with him.

Not that Ares needed it.

He was qualified.

More than qualified.

So are you.

She was. And she missed the work out in the field so much. She would like to be his partner out there, just like old times. Except she couldn't. She had to be responsible for Jeremy's sake. She just couldn't be selfish and put her career before her child. Her parents had done that, and look how that had turned out.

Wiping the sleep from her eyes, Pauly reluctantly left her warm bed and padded across the hall to wake up Jeremy. But when she got to his room, his bed was empty. The scent of fresh-brewed coffee and eggs came wafting up the stairs, making her stomach growl in appreciation.

She crept close to the stairs and could hear Ares and Jeremy laughing. It made her heart skip a beat. Jeremy was not an early riser. She practically had to drag him from bed and get him ready for school, yet he had beat her downstairs? What kind of sorcery was this?

Pauly grabbed her robe from her bedroom, cleaned herself up a bit and headed down. Jeremy was sitting at the island on a stool. He had a plate with eggs and fruit, even toast. It looked like a healthy breakfast. Usually, he'd groan if she tried to get him to eat anything but cereal.

"Good morning," she said brightly.

"Mom, you slept in," Jeremy teased.

"Hey, Moms can sleep in too," Ares chided.

"Not my mom," Jeremy groused. "She's up at the crack of dawn!"

"Oh, really?" Pauly asked. "And how would you know? You never get up."

Jeremy laughed. "Okay, but you're always up before me and I think that's pretty close to dawn."

"That's cause she's a mom. Although, she's always gotten up really early. When we were in college, she'd force your dad and me to get up too." Ares winked at her and cracked another egg in the bowl to scramble.

Jeremy was still giggling. "Yeah, Dad liked to sleep in too. I'm like him."

"You definitely are," Ares said, grinning.

It melted her heart to see Jeremy so happy and ready for the day.

Pauly tousled his hair. "I'm proud you're up and you're eating breakfast and not just cereal. You're actually eating eggs!"

"Uncle Ari told me to have a good breakfast in the morning. He said I had to eat eggs or bugs."

Pauly shot him a look and Ares shrugged as he grabbed a plate and set it down in front of her.

"Bugs?" she queried.

"That cereal he was eating is full of sugar," Ares chided. "A bug would be better. Do you want coffee?"

"Please. I'll also take eggs over bugs." Pauly laughed quietly to herself as Ares poured her a cup of coffee.

"I figured as much."

"Uncle Ari said bugs have protein."

Pauly paused midway through taking a sip of coffee, trying not to imagine that taste. It was Ares's turn to chuckle.

"Did you pack your lunch?" Pauly asked Jeremy, changing the subject from bugs so she could eat breakfast.

Jeremy nodded. "Yep. I'm ready for school."

"Wonders never cease," she murmured taking another sip of her coffee.

"He's ready," Ares said, cracking a couple of eggs into the frying pan. "And tonight, after dinner, I told him we'd go sledding,"

"Yes! I'm going to take him down the biggest hill. It's going to be awesome." Jeremy continued eating and he was grinning to himself, no doubt picturing the ride.

"So you threaten my son with bugs and then bribe him with sledding?" Pauly teased.

"Well, it worked for me. I had to eat bugs though." Ares slid the eggs on her plate. "Sorry, I should've asked how you wanted your eggs."

"You're making me breakfast," Pauly stated. "I don't care if you dyed them Easter egg colors, any way is awesome."

Ares cocked an eyebrow. "Really? Well, maybe I'll have to come up with some interesting concoctions, things I've had in other countries on my travels, and see what you think then."

"You're in for it now, Mom," Jeremy chuckled. "Bugs!"

"No bugs. I swear," Ares stated. "Jeremy, you done? Doesn't your bus come soon?"

"Yep. Can you walk me to the bus stop?" Jeremy asked, sliding off the stool at the counter.

"I can." Ares turned off the stove and followed Jeremy down the stairs to the front door, leaving Pauly alone to just enjoy a few moments to herself with the delicious breakfast and hot coffee.

She kind of felt bad that she hadn't gotten up before Ares and made him breakfast, but it was nice to have it made for her.

When her family and Rex's family had been

there on and off, they'd helped out as much as they could, pitching in so she could work and run errands, but she'd still tried to keep to a routine. She'd been the one getting Jeremy up and making sure his lunch was packed and he got on the bus. This simple act of Ares making her breakfast and coffee was so unexpected and very much appreciated. She couldn't remember the last time someone had done something like this for her.

Once she finished up breakfast, she cleaned up the kitchen, not that there was a huge mess. She then headed back upstairs to finish getting ready for the day. By the time she came down dressed in her uniform, Ares was back and had poured himself a coffee, reading something on his phone.

He didn't have his uniform yet, but that would change when they went to the station and got everything all set up.

"Thank you for cleaning up," Ares stated, as she came downstairs. "You didn't have to. I made the mess,"

"No, you cooked breakfast and got Jeremy out the door. That's kind of amazing!"

"Well, if I remember correctly Rex was never an early riser, unless food was involved. And Jeremy's a lot like his dad."

Pauly smiled. "I forgot you two were roommates before I moved in and straightened you both out."

Ares nodded. "He was also a terrible cook. The

times he beat me to the kitchen…well, I'd rather eat bugs."

Pauly giggled. "He did get better."

Ares looked at her in disbelief. "Really?"

"Okay, fine. He never did. It was terrible. He tried though."

There were so many times when she'd been suffering from morning sickness and Rex had tried to cook her something, anything, to get her to eat, but it just turned out to be disastrous. She couldn't quite figure out how he always managed to make batches of brownies that were simultaneously burnt *and* raw in the center.

"I knew it," Ares stated, finishing his cup of coffee and then putting the mug in the dishwasher. "So, are we ready to do this orientation? Also, I'm going to have to rent a car."

"Why?" Pauly asked.

"I can't have you drive me everywhere," Ares said. "You don't need to manage me, Pauly."

It threw her off for a second. "I guess I'm used to it. Managing people."

He smiled at her warmly. "I know. I remember, but I'm here to help you out. Besides, I'm a world traveler, over thirty, I can take care of myself."

She laughed softly. "Yes. That's true."

"So I'll rent a car."

"I still have Rex's car. I take it out from time to time. You can use that. It's in the garage." She honestly had thought a lot about selling it, but she was glad that she hadn't, because Ares was right. Once this training week was over they'd most likely be on different schedules and she couldn't drive him everywhere.

Just because he was here to help her out and be there for Jeremy for the year didn't mean that he didn't have freedom to pursue his own life. Go on a date or something.

Just thinking about that actually made her stomach knot a bit.

An intrusive shred of jealousy niggled at the back of her mind, surprising her.

He's not yours. He's just a friend.

"If you don't mind me using Rex's car, that would be great. I don't want to be a burden to you."

"Ares, you're far from a burden. If anything…" but she stopped herself from ending that sentence. It would have been something about how *she* didn't want to burden him or tie him down, especially when he was so adamant about his wandering life.

She never wanted to be a burden. She couldn't be that. She was a good daughter, reliable, dependable. She'd proved she was strong enough to look after herself, even at a tender age.

Except, you weren't.

There was a touch to her chin. She looked up to see Ares standing in front of her. His dark eyes were soft, making her heart race just a little at the kindness and tenderness there. At the realization that she could easily melt in that caring gaze of his. That she could really use a pair of strong arms wrapped around her, to comfort her. She missed that.

Rex would want you to be happy.

That was true. He would. But she wasn't going to ruin her friendship with Ares because she was lonely. She wouldn't risk losing what she and Ares had. Besides, Ares had made it clear in college, after his parents split up, that he had no interest in ever getting married and settling down. It was clear that Ares loved his life of traveling the world and exploring.

There was no way she would ever dream of shackling him down, and she had to protect Jeremy. She didn't want him to be hurt, to have another fatherlike figure taken from him. Even though Ares would fit so easily into her and Jeremy's life…

And what about you? Falling for someone who could be snatched from you again by a simple twist of fate?

Yeah, she wasn't putting her heart through that again.

"Pauly, you're not a burden. I'm here because I care for you and Jeremy. You are my best friend, and this is what friends do."

Pauly swallowed the lump in her throat, and

looked away. "Well, I appreciate it. We better get to the station house. It would look bad if you showed up to your first day late."

Ares nodded. "Lead on."

Pauly nervously tucked a strand of hair behind her ear and tried not to think about all those thoughts that had been running through her head. It was annoying that she was even giving them room in her mind. All she could do was chalk that up to loneliness.

But she was no stranger to isolation. She was used to it. So she was going to make sure she was more careful. The last thing she wanted to do was run Ares off early because he was scared of being tied down or couldn't handle her emotions.

She had to make sure he enjoyed his year here. He didn't need to shoulder anything. She could handle it.

If he left it would break Jeremy's heart and hers.

Ares was kicking himself for reaching out and touching her, just like he had last night, but when it came to Pauly he forgot himself. When Rex had been around it had been easier, because he'd never betray his best friend. He'd fought back the temptation.

He'd just felt so comfortable around her, he'd let down his guard. And now, as they drove to the station house, it was clear something had shifted. She had thrown up some kind of wall between them. He had to do better. Just because Rex was gone, there was no excuse. He still had no plans to ever marry or settle down, and Pauly deserved to be happy again with someone who wanted that.

Don't you deserve that too?

He shook that little thought from his mind.

He'd meant everything he'd just said to her.

She was his best friend. Rex had been too, but Rex was gone now, and Ares couldn't rely on his family much. There was too much turmoil there.

All he really had was Pauly and Jeremy, and there was no way that he was going to jeopardize it. Even if his heart was telling him otherwise.

"You okay?" he asked carefully, because he didn't want to make his first day working with her any weirder or more tense than it already would be after his slip at the house.

"Sure," Pauly said, glancing at him quickly.

"Hmm. Why don't I believe you?"

She smiled, her tense shoulders relaxing. "You know, I really hate you sometimes."

"I can read you quite clearly."

"You read me when it's convenient," she said, sardonically.

"How do you mean?"

"Like when I'd try and send you and Rex subliminal messages to study or clean up the apartment. You both seemed oblivious then."

"Okay, well, I've matured."

They both shared a look and laughed.

"It's training day and I guess I am worried about how you'll fit in."

Ares snorted. "You don't have to worry about me. I fit in anywhere. Anyway, I'm a big boy—I can take care of myself."

"Really?" she teased.

"What's that supposed to mean?"

"Well, there was that time you tried to clean the oven with dish detergent."

"It's soap!"

"You know if dish detergent burns, it releases toxins."

Ares groaned inwardly and scrubbed a hand over his face. "You would have to bring that up."

Pauly was still laughing as she pulled into the parking lot of the station house, a bright new building on the main road just outside of town. At least whatever tension was between them had melted away, and that was a very good thing indeed. He followed her out of her truck, and they headed in together. He wasn't nervous, but he was very aware that he was taking Rex's position. One that had been vacant since the accident two years ago.

Ares knew they were some pretty big shoes to fill.

This is the best job I've ever had, Ares," Rex remarked as they enjoyed a couple of beers on the deck overlooking the Three Sisters peak.

"You seem to love it," Ares agreed, taking a sip from his bottle. "Can't beat that view."

"No. You can't. You should move out here too."

Ares shook his head. "Nope. I like my wandering ways."

"Well, I can't wait to spend my career here, saving lives up on these mountains."

Ares glanced over at his friend and his far-off expression. The one of hope and realized dreams. Rex had it all. Beautiful wife, a son, and now his dream job.

Ares wasn't even sure of his dreams.

"Now you've gone a bit quiet," Pauly said, holding open the door.

"Have I?" he asked.

She nodded. "It'll be okay."

"I know. Lead the way." And he followed Pauly into the station house. There were a couple of ambulances in the bay as well as fire trucks. It was clean, well-kept and organized with their supplies.

So different from some of the places he worked. Towns and countries that had nothing. He was used to roughing it, so this would be like a vacation, sort of.

"What do you think?" Pauly asked.

"It's laid out well."

"We have a staff of fire, rescue, EMS and paramedics. Part-time, casual, full-time. We don't actually have any volunteers. We're fully trained."

She spoke with pride and he didn't blame her. It was a beautiful town and an impressive facility.

"And what area do we cover?" he asked, following her as she made her way through the main bay to what looked like a bunch of training rooms and offices, just past a large kitchen.

"We serve Canmore, but we offer aid to Big Horn and Kananaskis."

He nodded. "I'm eager to get started."

In particular, he couldn't wait to climb, but he wouldn't tell Pauly that. Admitting that he was excited to get out there on the mountains would cause her some anxiety. He knew that. She didn't know that he saw her flinch when he first talked about his gear being sent out. And he couldn't blame her for the idea of it bothering her. Rex had died on the mountain.

It was sweet she cared for Ares too, in a way none of his family ever had. He was so used to being on his own, with no one looking out for him. It was kind of nice.

"We'll get you a uniform, fill out your paperwork with human resources and then we'll head out on the trails. It's a gorgeous day with fresh snow, we'll do a patrol of one of the more easily accessible trails."

As much as Ares just wanted to get out there and throw himself into his work, he knew this kind of bureaucracy was just part of working in a town like this. Pauly took him to the human resources department and introduced him to some of the team, then left. She didn't need to stick around while he filled out all the paperwork, signed his life away on a contract and got everything set up so that he could work.

He was assigned a uniform and found the dormitory that was used by crews on a long shift to rest. It was a nice enough setup.

This was going to be a good year—he had to keep telling himself that. He wasn't used to staying in one place for so long. Often, if he stayed still for too long, he became restless. Being on the move didn't give him much time to think of things, like past regrets. He was worried that a year in the same place would definitely test his strength, especially when it came to Pauly.

It would be hard fighting his attraction, but he'd done it before. And he was doing this for her, and Jeremy. And, in a way, Rex. It would be worth it.

Once he had changed and put his street clothes in his assigned locker, he went to find Pauly in the main bay where she was waiting beside a couple of snowmobiles. He smiled seeing her with a clipboard, going over everything. He'd forgotten how cute she looked in a uniform. When they were in school, he and Pauly had been assigned to the same placement and had to wear uniforms as they job shadowed a paramedic in Toronto.

He particularly loved the way she looked in this uniform. It was just work clothes, nothing special, but somehow she looked adorable in the big work boots, straight pants, the no-nonsense navy shirt with yellow EMS patches on the sleeve and her hair pulled back in a tight bun.

It was difficult being in love with your best friend for years and knowing you could never have her.

It was a special kind of torture.

You need to get a grip, Ares.

"Hey," he said, approaching her. "We're going out on a trail?"

Pauly looked him up and down, ignoring his question. "Well, that uniform suits you."

"I had to tie my hair back," he remarked.

"You don't have a man bun so it's all good." There was a secret smile. "To answer your previous question, yes, we're going on a trail close to town. Have you ridden a snowmobile before?"

"No. Actually, I haven't."

"Oh." She worried her bottom lip. "We'll have to share one. Then we'll get you set up with lessons, because they're a useful tool for some of the trails around here."

"No doubt. I can ride a horse."

Her eyes went wide. "Well, that's good. Not the right season for the horses on the mountain trails, but that is good to know. I can let other mountain rescue teams in the area know that."

"Good."

"Well, we have snowsuits and helmets. I've

packed all the gear we need." She handed him a small binder. "This will have all the information about how the equipment is set up and what gear is recommended when out on the trails."

He flipped through it. "I'll study it."

"Yes. You can leave it on the bench there for when we get back."

"You're going to make me flash cards and quiz me, aren't you?" he mused sardonically.

"Maybe."

"You haven't changed a bit," he muttered as he followed her to grab the snowsuits and heavy boots. "So we're snowmobiling down the trail?"

"No. We have skis." Pauly pointed to what was strapped to the back in a little sledge that he hadn't noticed before. "We'll use the snowmobile to get to the trail head."

"Nordic skiing?"

She nodded. "Not many active snowmobile trails in Canmore, but out the back of this station is one that we can use as EMS. Then we'll ski through the groomed trail. It's a very popular sport."

Once they were suitably dressed, she opened the one back door. There was a trail from the back of the station house that led onto the main trail where they would be doing their training, so they didn't have to get the snowmobile onto a trailer and drag it somewhere, but Pauly explained that was what was usually done when they had to use the snowmobiles off trails when completing a search and rescue.

What was eating away at Ares right now was the fact that he was going to have to ride behind her. At least it was going to be a short ride. And he wouldn't have to wrap his arms around her. He could, but there was an option of handles on the back of the seat that he could grip.

And even though he wouldn't mind holding on to her, he really shouldn't tempt fate that way.

Pauly slipped on her helmet as the bay doors rose and started the engine. Ares climbed on behind her.

He wasn't exactly too thrilled about skiing either, but he understood he needed the training.

It had been a long time since he'd last skied, and he hadn't started until he was an adult. There'd been a time in his travels that he went with some colleagues to Gstaad and did some downhill skiing for the first time.

Even though he was Canadian, his family, especially his parents, weren't big on the winter outdoor fun activities. The only thing he'd done as a child had been some tobogganing with his brothers. That had led to some fast rides down some very icy hills and a few broken bones. Still, it was always a fun time and he was eager to take Jeremy sledding later. He'd been so excited when Ares had suggested it, which made Ares happy. It had been so long since he'd gone sledding, so to be able to do that with his godson was something he was really looking forward to. It was something special he and Jeremy could share and he wanted that special bond between them.

He wanted to be just more than a godfather in name. Jeremy needed him right now.

What about you? Don't you need him too?

The thought caught him off guard.

There was a part of him, deep down, that always wanted the kind of family he'd thought he had when he was growing up, before things turned sour. A wife, children. But he just didn't see how that was possible. How could he be a good father or husband? He didn't have the most stellar examples from his past.

When he looked back, he realized he'd barely seen his parents as a kid. They'd always been at the restaurant.

At least Jeremy was getting the childhood he deserved. Pauly made sure of that. She was a good mother and the more Ares thought about it, the more he realized there was so much to adore about her.

She was doing it on her own, and yet Jeremy had all the love and attention he needed. Something countless couples didn't manage to give their children, even with two of them. Like his parents.

A niggling little thought crept into Ares's mind. If Pauly could make it work, why couldn't he?

"Hold on," Pauly shouted over the hum of the engine.

He gripped the handles on the back of the snow-mobile tight as she navigated her way through the private trail, taking her time and slowing down at junctions where snowshoers and skiers might be crossing to connect to another trail. The sun was out and the mountains were glorious rising up into a clear blue sky. It was cold, and Ares was definitely missing the Caribbean and the warm sand, but there was beauty, even in a place where the air hurt your face.

Finally they got to the trail head and Pauly parked their machine. She took off her helmet and pulled her toque out of her pocket. "You ready?"

"To ski. Sure. To embrace this," he said, nodding at the snowmobile. "The jury is still out."

She smiled, but it was a sarcastic grin. There was a twinkle in her eyes.

Pauly deserved better than him. Someone who could give her the family life, grounded and rooted. Not somebody who was terrified of relationships because he really just couldn't let himself believe that they could work. And there was no way he ever wanted to be responsible for hurting her or Jeremy.

Focus on the work, he reminded himself.

He climbed off the snowmobile and they packed their helmets in the little hard-topped sledge. They pulled out their collapsible poles and goggles, then strapped on their skis.

Ares slid a bit, but he remembered the motion of gliding through the snow.

Maybe this will be okay.

"Come on. We'll do a run to the first junction and then back."

"Sure thing."

They set out on the trail. It was quiet. There were a few trees, but it was well groomed, with perfect grooves for the skis to slide through. Between the bright sun and the crisp white snow, he could see why so many people liked doing this. There was a connection to nature and even the mountain itself. It was quiet, just the sounds of the skis shushing through the snow.

He could get used to this.

It also gave him the perfect view of Pauly's backside.

Think about something else, Ares. Anything else.

Why did his brain keep betraying him? He was here to work, to help her out, not just lust over her. Again. She was off-limits.

"Help!" The shout echoed across the trail.

Pauly froze and he stopped to listen too.

"Help!" came the voice again.

Pauly pulled out her binoculars and scanned the area, but Ares saw it first—a tiny hand waving from beside the Bow River, well off the trail.

The riverbank was particularly steep and it might be deceptive to a tourist who was skiing.

"There, Pauly!" Ares guided her, by pointing.

"I see them. They're on the riverbank." She put her binoculars away. "You have the EMS kit in your backpack, right?"

He nodded. "I do."

"Okay, let's go. Looks like you get a crash course on training day."

Ares followed Pauly off the groomed trail. The snow was deeper and harder to ski through, but this was what he was trained for.

To save lives.

CHAPTER FIVE

PAULY HADN'T BEEN in the field for so long, and now the rush she was feeling as she and Ares made their way over to where they heard the call for help was all adrenaline.

It reminded her of why she became a paramedic. One of the reasons.

"You're okay, sweetie," the woman paramedic said, gently wrapping her up in a blanket after the fireman had rescued her. "We're going to check you over now and make sure you're okay."

Pauly nodded, coughing. "I wasn't meant to start the stove. But my brother was hungry and Dad was late. I forgot to turn it off when they got home."

"It's all right. Your parents explained."

"I have to take care of Sam," Pauly explained.

"Your brother is fine." The paramedic set her down on the gurney, instantly calming her as they checked her over.

That paramedic had taken care of her. The early part of her childhood and adolescence, she'd taken care of her younger brother, Sam. After the fire, things changed with her family. Things had gotten better. Her parents didn't work so much. Her grandma took her and Sam for a while and then moved in with them when they went back to their parents. Pauly was no longer alone, though she'd still struggled with nightmares and panic attacks. But one good thing she'd gleaned from it all was that she knew without a doubt what she wanted to do. She wanted to help others.

Still, it was hard to be out here. What was supposed to be a simple training session was now something real and dangerous.

Pauly, they need you.

She locked away all the anxiety to focus on what she was trained to do. There was no way she was turning her back on people in need.

As they got closer she could see where the two skiers had become stuck. There wasn't usually this much snow by the beginning of November. It was still a little bit warmer compared to when he arrived and windy, and the snow had drifted in a false ledge over a steep bank of the Bow River, giving the false impression that it was solid, when actually it was hollow. As soon as the skiers had stepped on it, it must have caved in, dropping them down the bank, where they were precariously trying to stay out of the rushing, icy cold water below.

It wasn't a particularly long drop, but the frigid

weather and cold water would mean that hypothermia would set in.

Fast.

"Be careful," Pauly shouted over her shoulder to Ares. "It's not as solid as it looks."

"Where's the riverbank?" Ares asked, coming up beside her.

"There are markers." Pauly pointed them out. "It's quite steep here."

"What're the coordinates?" Ares asked, pulling out the radio that connected to the fire station.

"Right here," she handed him the map of the trail. "Get them to send a rig to the Ascension Bridge."

Ares nodded and made the call while she dug through for a rope and some crampons.

"Help," the person called again. "Not sure how long we can keep holding on!"

"Help is on the way," Pauly responded. "Are you injured?"

"I think my friend is. They're tied to me, but they're unconscious and I'm worried about them falling into the river."

Pauly found it interesting that the two skiers were tied together, but since they'd gone off trail and had the snow pack crumble beneath then, it was a blessing. The rope might've saved their lives. How could they have been so careless, putting their lives at risk?

That's not important now.

She took her time to assess where the edge was and how she could approach a rescue without the snow giving way underneath her too. Her pulse was pounding in her ears and she couldn't quite figure it all out. All she could think about was how dangerous it was.

"Let me go," Ares said, after finishing his call to the station.

"You don't know the river."

"I don't know a lot of rivers and I've still done fast water rescues before. And rescues in mudslides and avalanches. I can do this." He pulled out the neoprene suit from the gear and started pulling it on over his winter gear.

"Okay," Pauly agreed.

She didn't argue with him. There wasn't any time, and she was second-guessing herself a bit, which annoyed her. She hated that hesitation, but all she could think of in the moment was Rex and Jeremy. What if something happened to her? The idea of leaving Jeremy orphaned was something she couldn't contemplate.

This was what she'd trained for. This is what she dedicated her life to doing, saving others. She was good at it.

Everything will be fine.

It was hard to believe that when she assessed the precariousness of this whole situation. Her pulse was pounding between her ears, her throat dry as she just ran through all the most terrible scenarios in her head.

You have to stop.

She trusted Ares, but if anything happened to him under her watch... Well, her stomach knotted just picturing it. All she could think about was how she couldn't save Rex, how crushed Jeremy would be if something happened to Ares or her.

How devastating it would be to lose Ares.

Her body trembled.

She thought she was ready to go back in the field. Maybe she'd been wrong.

Breathe. This will all be okay.

She took a deep calming breath to ground herself back in the present, and shook those niggling thoughts of self-doubt from her mind. There was no place for them here as she continued to help Ares get ready, so they could start the rescue before the rig arrived. She knew it wouldn't take long for the rest of the team to get there; she just wasn't sure if these two skiers had that long in them.

Ares hadn't been lying—he seemed to know exactly what he was doing as he approached the riverbank cautiously from the side, making sure to break a path so that he didn't lose his footing with the crumbling snow.

Thankfully, the whole riverbank wasn't as precarious. The two they were trying to rescue had just been unfortunate. Watching Ares work was awe-inspiring, but it also called up a flash of panic.

It hit her so hard.

Please. Keep him safe.

Rex had *died*, doing this job, up the mountain.

She tried to focus on her own work, forcing an anchored post through the snow into the not-quite-frozen ground, something they could use to help them hoist the skiers to safety. But she couldn't stop turning to watch Ares as he threw out a line to the conscious skier, then made his way slowly to cut the tie between the two and secure the un-conscious patient., All she could think back to was that moment she heard what had happened to her husband. It played over and over again in her mind.

Her stomach was in knots as she paced the station house. At least Jeremy was safe with the sitter, but she'd heard the rumbles and she knew Rex and the team were on the mountain when the avalanche hit.

So many avalanches for December.

As she waited to hear about the team, the chief motioned for her to join him in his office.

"Have a seat, Pauly," Pierre said, gently.

Her insides churned, her whole world dropping out beneath her like she was free-falling without a parachute. It was Pierre's tone, his sympathetic expression. As she sat down numbly in the chair, she knew, her husband was gone.

But this wasn't Rex. This wasn't the mountain. It was all right.

She took another deep breath to steady her shaking hands, waiting in anticipation for Ares to give her the all clear.

"Okay, Pauly. I've secured the second patient, pull the other up," he called out.

"All right," she acknowledged. She secured the rope around the anchored post, then used her body weight, sitting back into the snow bank and digging her heels in so that she could help the first skier up.

The rope just guided the conscious victim and gave him a little extra push as Pauly verbally encouraged him to crawl up the bank to safety. Once he was up on the solid bank and out of harm's way, Pauly helped him stand. She could feel him trembling and knew he was cold—he'd been hanging on for some time.

"It's okay," Pauly reassured him. "I've got you."

The man didn't respond with words, just an exhausted nod of acknowledgement. The rest of the team had arrived as she'd been hoisting, and they rushed over with a stretcher, ready to assist. Pauly was so focused on her patient, that it was a moment before she remembered Ares, still helping the unconscious skier back up the bank of the river.

"Ares?" she called out. Her pulse was thundering between her ears because she couldn't see him. She'd lost track of him.

All these horrible thoughts ran through her head. What if he slipped? What if he was in the river?

Picturing him hurt or injured made it a bit harder to breathe.

Just calm down. It'll be okay.

Only she didn't know that.

The idea of losing her best friend was too much to bear. Worst-case scenarios circled around and around in her head.

That had never happened before, back when she started her career. She and Ares had done a lot of their co-op and placements together in school, and not once had she worried about him. But now she had this existential dread filling her mind, her chest, and all she could do was hold her breath, placing her hands over her heart, waiting.

Then she saw an arm wrap around the rope at the bank, and Ares came up, the unconscious skier tied to his waist. The breath Pauly hadn't known she was holding released as relief washed through her. She carefully approached the edge and helped Ares as they got the other skier onto solid snow and another stretcher was brought over.

"Unconscious female. Appears to have hit her head on a rock," Ares rattled off as the rest of the team worked over the woman. "There was blood. One pupil is dilated, but the patient is still breathing. Their lower extremities were in the water, so I suspect hypothermia as well as a concussion."

Pauly threw herself into the work, but it was easier now. She felt better knowing that they had saved the two stranded skiers and both she and Ares were okay. All that worry was melting away.

They got the two patients loaded while an RCMP officer came to get their statement. Unfortunately, the two victims of this accident had been skiing off the groomed trail where there was clearly posted signs and they would face some fines.

Once that was all done, they loaded up their equipment in the back of the patrol car and the RCMP officer got Ares and Pauly back to the snowmobile so they could return to the station house.

Neither of them really said anything, which was kind of a relief because Pauly was still so confused about her reaction out there in the field. She was mad at herself for letting those worries creep through her mind, immobilize her.

Maybe this going back to work in the field wasn't going to be as easy as she thought.

That worried her, because she loved her job. It was the one thing she had left, but she couldn't do her job effectively if she was terrified. And today watching Ares put his life on the line had scared her.

And then there was Jeremy. The thought of

leaving him alone cut her to the quick. She knew all too well what that was like. And suddenly she felt like that little girl version of herself. The child who had to grow up far too quickly.

That wasn't what she wanted for Jeremy.

Ever.

That was the thought playing over and over in her mind as they rode the snowmobile the short way back to the station house.

"You look worried," Ares said, a question in his voice, as they took off their winter gear to be dried.

"Do I?" she asked absently.

He gave her a look of disbelief. "Really? Come on, Pauly how long have we known each other?"

A wry laugh escaped her. "True. Okay, I was a bit worried."

"About?"

She sighed and sat down on the bench as she finished removing her winter boots. "I had a moment of panic, when I couldn't see you."

His brow furrowed. "What?"

"I know. It was my first day back out in the field and… I don't know what came over me. I just kept thinking about…" She sighed again and wrapped her arms around herself. "I kept thinking about Rex and Jeremy. It's been two years and it's still affecting me. It's silly."

"No. It's not. Those feelings are valid."

She shook her head. "How can I do my job if I'm worrying like this?"

Ares squatted down in her front of her. His warm eyes stared up at her and he placed his hands on her arms. It was comforting, it was nice and it grounded her instantly.

"You will get there. Of course you're going to have anxiety after what happened to Rex. Give yourself some grace in this situation." His words were soft and tender. They were exactly what she needed in that moment. Something she had been missing for some time.

Rex had known about her childhood, but Ares didn't. Anxiety was something she'd worked hard to manage her whole life. It was hard to do that when your rock was gone. She hadn't had that security in a long time now and all the while she had to be that safe harbor for Jeremy. She appreciated Ares being there for her. For understanding.

"Thanks."

"It'll be okay. I promise you. You better not give up because of one moment of uncertainty."

"I won't." Her voice shook, but all that worry and tension she had been feeling because of that rush of anxiety in the field was beginning to melt away. She was so glad Ares was here. She wanted to get back to work. She wanted to find a sense of normalcy again, her confidence. She wanted to feel something other than grief and this survival mentality that she had been operating in the past two years.

She wanted to live again.

"Good." Ares stood and then held out his hand to help her up.

She slipped her hand in his and he helped her to her feet. They were close together and she looked up at him. Suddenly her heart was racing again, but now it was with something different.

Quickly, Pauly took a step back. As much as she wanted to get back to a normal life, she wasn't quite sure that she wanted *that* much normalcy, no matter how lonely she was or how much Ares meant to her.

There was no way she was going to jeopardize their friendship.

Not for anything.

"Well," she said, clearing her throat. "You have some more training modules to complete and I have some paperwork to file thanks to the impromptu rescue operation that happened today during your training, which we didn't really get to complete."

Ares nodded. "Right."

"I'll be heading back home about five. Jeremy is staying with his sitter until then, so after our shift we have to pick him up."

"Sounds good. How about we have dinner somewhere tonight?" he asked. "Grab Jeremy and just celebrate our first day of working together. Which I think was definitely calmer than the first time."

"What do you mean?" she asked, crossing her arms.

He laughed. "You were ready to murder me after our first job placement together. You said I kept getting in the way."

"Why are you mad, Paul?" Ares asked.

"Ugh, because you were constantly doing everything."

Ares looked confused. "What?"

"I'm learning too. I can do stuff too. You don't have to do everything." Pauly took a deep breath. "Sorry, I'm frustrated. It seemed like the paramedics were ready to trust you, but overlooked me. Sorry I blamed you there."

"Ah," Ares said, then he smiled warmly. "You're too quiet, Paul. Not with me, but with them. You have to speak up. Fight for it, for the opportunity."

"Even if it means fighting you?" she questioned in a half tease.

"Especially me." He winked at her.

Pauly laughed. "I'd forgotten that."

"Figures," he grunted. "Remember how Rex made us all go out to dinner and settle the differences with a game of pool?"

"Well, we could go bowling tonight," Pauly suggested. "Jeremy would love that. I wouldn't mind skipping tobogganing."

"Ditto. I've had enough snow and cold today. Will Jeremy mind?" Ares asked.

"Nope."

Ares nodded. "That sounds like fun. And I think you need some fun tonight."

"You're right. I do."

"Good. I'll see you later, boss." Ares saluted and left the ambulance bay.

Pauly sighed nervously and finished cleaning up her gear. It was nice to have Ares around, but she was surprised at how much emotion he was stirring up, how many forgotten memories.

But they were all *good* memories.

And she had to remember that it was only temporary.

After the excitement down by the river the rest of Ares's day was boring. He hated paperwork and all the human resource stuff that he had to go through. This was the reason he liked traveling all over the world and working in places that a lot of others in his line of work didn't get to. His whole reason for becoming a paramedic was to help people, *that* was what he liked. This morning, he'd really enjoyed being able to help those two stranded skiers.

Sitting in a meeting room and going through the endless new-hire stuff, on the other hand, was putting him to sleep and making him a bit squirrelly. What he had to remind himself of was that he was doing this to help Pauly and Jeremy.

He was doing this for Rex.

Honestly, he'd always envied Rex for what he had, even if Ares had spent most of their college lives telling everyone who would listen that, with his messed-up family, he *never* wanted to settle down He'd had multiple girlfriends over the years... Well, he couldn't even really call them that—they were more like one-night stands. His longest-lasting relationship was maybe a week.

None of those times had made him truly happy.

The truth was, there was a part of him that wanted something more. Something real, but he was terrified of what could happen if it didn't work out. He didn't want to have kids involved in the breakup of a marriage. He knew what that was like. Even though he'd been in college when his parents had split, able to look out for himself, he'd seen how his brothers' failed marriages had hurt his nieces and nephews.

Clearly, his family was cursed or something.

Yet, when he saw Pauly, Rex and Jeremy, he knew it could work out, for some people. There was happiness there. There was love and he wanted that. Secretly, he wanted all of it, but there was no way he was going to jeopardize anything to achieve that.

It was better to just stay Pauly's friend and be there for Jeremy, because if something went wrong and he lost them, it would devastate him. He didn't want to lose more of his family.

Only, it was hard to keep reminding himself of that promise he had made to himself. Especially, when he was working alongside Pauly again.

It felt like it did all those years ago.

And as he stared at the module on the computer screen, another silly test that the station's HR department was making him take, his mind wandered to all the fun times that Pauly and he shared when they had been doing the portion of their schooling working on the job as students. All the nutty things they'd seen. All the jokes they'd shared.

She belonged to Rex though.

That niggly little voice was back again, reminding him that no matter how much fun they had together, when it was just the two of them, she always went back home to Rex. Always was in Rex's arms in their shared apartment.

Pauly had never been his. And she wasn't his now.

Ares groaned and scrubbed his hands over his face as he glanced at the clock. It was ten to five and he was just thankful that this day was almost over. When he sat idly or sat and did paperwork his mind would always dwell on things that he really didn't want to contemplate, like Pauly.

At least tonight Jeremy would be there, and Ares could focus on his godson. It was good to spend time with him, see him smiling again, though he knew Jeremy was still grieving his father.

Ares still remembered the day of the memorial every time he looked at him.

He found Jeremy sitting alone while Pauly greeted guest after guest. They had just come back from spreading Rex's ashes on the mountain.

Jeremy had slipped out of the house and was idly swinging on his tire swing, his feet trailing slowly through the dirt.

"Hey," Ares said, gently.

"Hi, Uncle Ari," Jeremy responded half-heartedly.

"How are you?"

Jeremy shrugged. "Dunno."

"Can I sit with you awhile?"

Jeremy nodded and looked up at him. "It hurts."

"Yes. It will."

"You were his best friend right, Uncle Ari?"

"I am. Always will be. I'd like to be yours too."

Jeremy smiled. "Me too."

"Hey," Pauly said, interrupting his thoughts.

"Yeah?"

"You ready to go?" she asked.

"Sure," he responded, shutting down the module. "I can finish the rest later at home."

"You don't sound too sure," she teased.

"I loathe paperwork," he grumbled.

"Right. All part of the job. And here I thought you were thinking about how I'm going to kick your butt at bowling." There was a glint in her eye as she said it. He'd forgotten that Pauly was slightly competitive.

Actually, that was a complete understatement.

She was really competitive, bordering on the annoying side.

For someone so sweet, she was kind of ruthless.

"Seriously? Kick my butt? You're a mother, you should know better," he teased.

Pauly rolled her eyes. "Come on, really? A mother? That's a pathetic attempt to curtail my awesomeness."

"It wasn't an attempt to curtail anything. You're super competitive and you know it," he countered.

"Like when?"

"Oh, like when you threw darts at my head because I beat your score."

She opened her mouth to say something else. "Fine. I promise I'll behave because Jere will be there."

"Hmm, why don't I believe you?" Ares followed her out of the boardroom. He grabbed his stuff from his locker. They were going to go home and change, then pick up Jeremy to have dinner at this restaurant that also had a bowling alley. It was a place to get a good meal and have fun bowling—or glow bowling, as Pauly had called it. It sounded very different from the bowling allies he used to frequent in his hometown of Whitby, where there were a lot of middle-aged men, tacky eighties decor and the lingering smell of smoke and feet in the air.

The place they were going definitely sounded more upscale. He had no doubt that Pauly still was going to be completely obnoxious about winning or losing, but that was fine by him, because for all her goodness, that one flaw she had made her even more endearing.

I have got to stop thinking about her this way. They were friends and nothing more.

CHAPTER SIX

ARES HAD BEEN bowling as a kid, but he couldn't remember *ever* bowling with his family. His dad had always been so focused on work, not his home life, which in retrospect might've been the problem between him and his mother all along.

The more Ares thought about it over the years, the more he saw of his brothers, the more he realized how similar they were to their dad. They worked too much and didn't spend time with their families, their kids. And Ares knew he was so dedicated to work, as well. Just another reason not to settle down.

Except...he liked spending time with Pauly and Jeremy. They'd had to drive over an hour to reach the alley. Pauly had acknowledged that it was a trek just for bowling, but there just wasn't a place like this in Canmore.

Canmore had a lot, but not this retro-inspired, neon-fueled, glow-in-the-dark bowling alley that he had been dragged to. As soon as they'd stepped inside, Jeremy had completely forgotten about tobogganing and Ares was more than okay with that. As much as he loved the mountains, and even though he wanted to share the experience of sledding with Jeremy, he didn't really feel like frolicking in the snow tonight. Not after the freezing river rescue earlier.

Jeremy was practically bouncing-off-the-walls excited by the time they were assigned their lane, which had a vinyl booth and a place for them to have their wood oven pizza while playing their game. It looked like a fifties diner, but with bad shoes and the crash of pins echoing.

"This is great!" Jeremy announced, lacing up his ugly bowling shoes. "I'm going to pick out a neon green ball."

"Why neon green?" Ares asked, curious only because it was so specific.

"'Cause it's cool," Jeremy responded in a tone like Ares was clueless or something.

"Well, I guess it sounds cooler than puce," Ares teased.

Jeremy's use wrinkled. "Puke?"

"Puce," Pauly corrected, laughing softly.

"Don't you think neon green is kind of…snot-colored?" Ares asked, knowing it would bug Pauly. But who else was going to teach Jeremy all the immature, gross stuff, all the laughs that he knew Rex would have shared with his son.

"Gross, guys," Pauly said while Jeremy chuckled wildly.

"No, Uncle Ari! It's *not* booger-colored. Neon is cool. I'm going to go get it." Jeremy leaped up.

"Nothing too heavy!" Pauly called after Jeremy as he went to pick out his ball from the rack. "Thanks for the booger talk, Ares," she groused, but he could see the twinkle in her eyes.

"I'd say I'm sorry, but I'm not."

"I know you're not. Put your shoes on." She handed him the bowling shoes.

"You'd think a place like this would have better-looking shoes," Ares grumbled tying his bowling shoes.

"I think it's sort of part of the experience of bowling," Pauly remarked. "You have to have ugly shoes."

Ares grunted, but they shared a smile which made his pulse race. "I suppose so."

"Just think about it this way, you're not throwing yourself down an icy hill in bitter cold weather."

"That's the bonus." He stood up. "Though I am looking forward to doing that with Jeremy. I loved it as a kid."

"Yeah, but now you're over thirty. It's not the same as when we were kids."

"I'm not decrepit."

She laughed. "I know, I'm just saying it's a bit… tiring."

"That I will agree with you on. Now, do you want me to grab some balls?"

Pauly's eyes went wide and her lips trembled with a badly contained smile. "Pardon?"

Ares realized what he'd said, and how it could be completely misconstrued. "I mean bowling balls. Jeez, Pauly, are you twelve or something?"

She laughed. "Okay, but come on! That is not something I ever thought you would say."

"Not usually." He couldn't help but think about what he'd rather get his hands on, but he kept that thought to himself, much like he'd always done when it came to Pauly.

"Sure, you can pick out a bowling ball for me," she teased. "Pink, definitely not blue."

He groaned and rolled his eyes. "Pink it is."

He walked over to the rack, passing Jeremy as he clutched his green bowling ball to his chest and walked back to their lane. Ares chuckled to himself, then picked out a pink ball and a yellow one for himself. He wanted to pick the blue ball, because then maybe Pauly would be too busy laughing at her immature little joke and choke on the game, but he decided to be nice.

He took the balls back to the lane and set them on the ball return next to Jeremy's neon-colored one, which was, thankfully, a better green than he'd been anticipating. Not a booger in sight.

Jeremy was back in the booth bouncing up and down as Pauly was ordering pizza from the waitress that had come to the lane. When he made his way back, the young woman smiled at him and batted her eyelashes. It was an obvious invitation to flirt—Ares was more than used to that.

He smiled back politely and nodded. It wasn't that she wasn't perfectly nice-looking, but she wasn't Pauly. Which had also been the problem for most of his adult life.

No one ever held a candle to her.

Pauly had a strange look on her face, like she was biting back a mischievous grin.

Oh. Great.

Ares knew what that look meant. She was going to try and set him up, just like she had in the past.

"Um, what do you want to drink, *Uncle* Ari?" It was pointed, the way she said *uncle*. He didn't like that she was calling him that, not in this instance anyway. She might as well have said *unattached*.

"I'm getting a chocolate milk," Jeremy exclaimed.

"I'll have an iced tea," Ares answered. "Thank you."

"Sure," the waitress said. "I'll be back in a few with your order."

Ares was not here to date and Alberta wasn't his home. In fact, he didn't have much of a home. There really wasn't time to even entertain a fling here. He was here for his best friend.

"She was cute," Pauly hinted. "She was totally blushing when you walked over."

Ares shrugged. "I suppose."

Jeremy was coloring on the kids paper place mat, completely oblivious to them.

"You know," Pauly said, "we never talked about your social life while you're here for the year."

"Pauly, I'm not interested in dating. You know that," he replied, flatly.

"But…"

"No," Ares stopped her quickly. "I don't have plans to settle down. My job takes me all over the world. Actually, this is the longest I'm staying still in one place, ever."

"Fine," she said, quietly. There was a strange expression on her face, but only for a moment, then it was gone. "I just don't want you to feel like you're stuck."

"I'm not stuck. Far from it. I want to be here with you and Jeremy." He reached across the table and took her hand, giving it a squeeze as their eyes locked. Her hand was so soft and tiny in his and he held on to it for longer than he should.

Sure, he'd dated in the past, but it was only ever casual because he never wanted to settle down. He liked his freedom.

Do you? How much?

"Can we play a game before the pizza comes?" Jeremy asked.

Ares let go of Pauly's hand, quickly. "Sure, buddy. You going to go first?"

"Yep."

Ares slid out of the booth so Jeremy could get

out, then followed him to the lane, watching over his godson as he picked up the ball, slipping his little fingers into the three holes and walking up to the painted line. He looked like some kind of professional.

"You know how to throw?" Ares asked, impressed.

"Yeah, Mom taught me." Jeremy let the ball go. Ares stood back, watching that neon green ball roll painfully slowly down the polished wooden lane, before it finally took one pin out at the end.

Well, so much for the pro bowler theory, Ares mused.

He glanced over his shoulder at Pauly who was clapping and cheering her son on. It warmed his heart to be here with her and Jeremy. He kept telling himself over and over again that he never wanted to commit to anyone or plant roots, but when he was here with them he forgot all that.

His parents had been in love once before it all went wrong and yeah, Ares had already spent a lot of years putting his career first, just like his dad. What if his life was destined to go the same way? He just couldn't take that risk with Pauly or with Jeremy. They didn't need heartbreak. They deserved better.

Better than him.

He didn't want Jeremy to ever experience that kind of pain that he went through, that his family continued to go through. The estrangement from his father hurt him to his very core. His family was broken.

So even if he secretly wanted all of this—family, togetherness, happiness, love—he just couldn't have it. He couldn't risk it, because he just didn't know what the future would bring and he really didn't believe in a fairy-tale happy ending, because most fairy tales he knew hadn't ended so happy.

Pauly wasn't sure why she'd suggested that Ares could date. It was obvious that the waitress found Ares attractive. In fact, most women did, and Pauly definitely didn't dispute that fact. The first time Rex had introduced her to Ares, she'd been kind of taken aback at how handsome he was, but he'd made it clear time and time again that he wasn't interested in anything long-term.

He liked his life.

Ares was carefree and had a wandering soul. There were times she envied his freedom and how much he traveled. She was glad he was here with her this year.

So she didn't understand the sudden drive to push him to date. Maybe, deep down, she wanted to protect herself and keep the temptation of falling for him at an arm's length, because it would be easier to put the idea out of her head if he was with someone else.

Would it, though?

She'd been relieved when he told her he wasn't interested in dating anyone, when it really shouldn't matter to her at all.

"Pauly, you're up," Ares called out, waving her over.

"Right." She put all those thoughts about Ares, dating, everything out of her mind. She was hating the idea that it kept popping up time and time again. The most important thing right now was to focus on having fun with her family.

But that thought also gave her pause, because they weren't a family.

Not really.

Ares is family, though, in a way. He always has been.

She picked up her bright pink ball. As she got under the black light of the lane, Ares smiled at her. His teeth were so extra white that she couldn't help snort-laughing a bit. Jeremy scampered off to watch his ball return up the shoot.

"What?" Ares asked, glancing over his shoulder.

"Your teeth are so white in this light. It's hard to concentrate. It's blinding."

He crossed his arms. "So are yours. They're glowing."

She quickly shut her mouth, pressing her lips together tightly. "You're just trying to sabotage me."

"Ha!" he barked with laughter. "Always so suspicious. There's a reason for that!"

"Oh?" she asked.

"Only competitive cheaters think everyone is out to get them."

"Cheaters?" she asked in mock outrage. "I can beat you with my eyes closed."

He cocked an eyebrow. "Oh, really? Show me then. Walk up to the line and close your eyes."

"Don't you think that's dangerous?"

"How? You roll it down the lane."

"What if I throw it at someone?"

Ares glanced around. "No one is next to us on either side. Are you telling me you're so strong you're going to shot put it at someone's head?"

"Maybe," she teased.

He rolled his eyes. "I'll guide you. Get up to the line and I'll make sure you don't take someone's head off."

Pauly went to the line at the start of the lane and closed her eyes. She could feel Ares come up behind her, his arms slip over hers as she held the ball up. His breath was hot on her neck and her body trembled a bit.

This was a mistake.

Only she didn't pull away. It felt so good.

"You ready?" he asked softly against her ear. The fan of his hot breath against her neck sent a rush of heat through her, making every nerve in her body light up in anticipation.

For what? A part of her wanted to ask, only she kept that to herself. His strong hands slid over her arms, leaving a trail of gooseflesh under his fingertips. Honestly, it was nice to have the arms of someone she trusted around her again. It was comforting.

In this moment she felt safe again and it hit her she hadn't felt like this in a long time.

"You ready?" he asked again, shifting his weight, her back pressed against his hard chest.

"Yep," she managed to squeak out.

"Okay. It's safe, let it go."

Pauly pushed back and he stepped away as she let the ball go down the lane. She could hear the rumble of it against the wooden floor and she opened her eyes as the pink ball headed straight down the lane, dead center, to the first pin— knocking them all down with a loud crash.

"Wahoo! A strike." She threw a fist in the air and spun around, but as she did the spin her bowling shoes slipped on the polished floor and she fell forward. Ares reached out, catching her and steadying her, just as her hands, bracing for the impact of the fall, hit him in the chest. She could feel his heart racing under the palms of her hands as he righted her, and she gazed up at him. Her breath caught in her throat, her body thrumming.

"You okay?" he asked.

"Fine," she said quickly, but she didn't step out of his embrace. She didn't want to, so she lingered, enjoying the moment.

"Well," he said. "I guess you've proven me wrong."

She laughed. "I guess so."

They just stood there for a few moments, staring at each other. Her pulse thundered between her ears as she got lost in his dark eyes. It was taking everything in her not to reach out and run her fingers through his hair.

Get a grip on yourself, girl.

"John!" someone screamed.

Pauly jumped back and they both looked down the bowling alley to the people three lanes from theirs.

There was a man lying on the floor, having what looked like a seizure. Instantly, Ares took off like a shot and Pauly went to be with Jeremy who looked scared.

"Mom, you have to go help," Jeremy said, clinging to her.

"You going to be okay?" Pauly asked, not wanting to leave him by himself.

"I will, Mom. I'll stay in the next lane. I can see you from there."

Pauly kissed the top of Jeremy's head and ran off with Ares. She looked back to see Jeremy climbing into the booth of the lane next to the man on the ground.

Ares was talking to the woman who had called out the man's name, telling her that they were paramedics and that she needed to call emergency services. Pauly did an assessment of John's airway and breathing. He was coming out of his seizure, his movements were relaxing, but Pauly could see that his fingernails were slightly blue and his body was still rigid.

"Help me get him on his side, Pauly," Ares instructed.

She nodded and scooted over, helping Ares to gently roll him on his side. There was a contusion on the back of John's head from where he had fallen, and it was bleeding steadily.

"I need some napkins," Pauly called out. She was handed a stack of napkins so she could apply pressure to the head wound.

Ares was busy loosening the buttoned collar of the man's shirt and checking his breathing again.

"John," Ares called softly. "John, let us know you're okay."

Only John wasn't waking, which wasn't surprising after a seizure. It took a lot out of a person.

"How is his breathing?" Pauly asked.

"Still good. And his head?" he asked.

"It's deep and he needs to get a CT scan. It seems he hit his head hard on this floor."

It wasn't long before the Calgary paramedics came in and they got John loaded up onto the gurney to head to the hospital. Pauly went to wash her hands as Ares spoke with the paramedics. When she came back John's party was breaking up and Ares was standing with Jeremy. The waitress who had been openly flirting with Ares was standing at their booth waiting patiently.

"I think our pizza is ready," Pauly said, her voice shaking as the adrenaline was running out. "You guys hungry?"

Jeremy nodded. "Yep. You both did awesome."

Ares smiled down at Jeremy and tousled his head. "You're a good kid."

Jeremy shrugged. "I know."

Pauly shook her head in mirth and walked back to their lane and sat down. Although suddenly she wasn't very hungry. Just exhausted as her body came down off that high of helping another. And she was proud of how Jeremy handled himself, especially in that tense situation.

"Every time we're together something seems to happen," Ares remarked.

"What do you mean?" she asked.

"Halloween, training…now this." He gestured where John had been. "Like I'm being tested."

"Maybe, but I'm glad we were here to help him."

Ares nodded. "Me too."

They finished their pizza, their game and then headed back to the truck. It was a clear night, and they got a very tired Jeremy loaded and buckled up. As soon as they hit the Trans-Canada Highway to head back to Canmore, Jeremy was asleep in the back.

"He's out like a light," Ares remarked.

"I could easily nap too."

"It's been a lot of excitement," Ares said as they drove west out of the city and into the foothills toward the mountains.

"It has," she said, quietly. "He's so happy you're here."

"I'm happy to be here," Ares replied. "How about you?"

"What do you mean?"

"Are you happy I'm here?"

"Why wouldn't I be?"

Ares shrugged. "I don't want to step on your toes and invade your space."

"You're not. I want you here, Ares. I'm so glad you're here." And she quickly glanced at him. "I just don't want to hold you back from your life."

"Is that why you brought up me dating while I'm here."

"I suppose so."

"Well, you're not holding me back. Besides, what life do I have?"

"Traveling?"

He scoffed. "I mean it's fun, but... I don't have a wife or kids. I don't have family that misses me. I have no roots or connection."

"Isn't that what you always wanted since your parents' split?"

"Yes," he responded, quietly. "Still, I get... lonely. It's weird not having family."

"Do you not talk to your parents, your siblings?"

He shrugged. "My mom, yes, but my brothers and my sister are busy with their lives and their work and Dad and I...we haven't spoken in years."

Pauly sighed. She knew it had been hard for Ares when his parents split up and that he didn't like to talk about it much, but she thought by now that he and his father would've patched things up. She and Ares shared so much, but there were still things she really didn't know about him. Things he kept close to his chest. Just like she did. It was like he didn't trust the world around him.

Do you?

It was hard for her to trust the world, because she wasn't sure that she was back in it. She was still kind of mad over losing Rex. Life was cruel sometimes, infinitely so. Fate too.

It hurt, a raw pain, even after all this time.

"Wow," Ares gasped, breaking her silent rumination.

"What?" she asked, looking out ahead of her.

"Pull over at the rest stop," Ares instructed.

She didn't question and pulled over on the small turnoff that was used mainly by long-haul truckers on the highway to rest. It was basically a parking lot, with endless open fields on either side and a couple of port-a-potties. She parked her truck.

"What're we doing?" she asked.

"Turn off the car and then step out."

Pauly gave him a quizzical look, but did what he asked. Ares climbed out and then Pauly slid out of the truck, locking it and coming to stand beside him. He was staring up at the dark clear sky to the north.

"You know, this is how those old urban legends about men with hook hands start," she teased.

"Just look and let your eyes adjust," he said, impatiently.

"Fine." She crossed her arms and gazed where he was looking. As her eyes adjusted to the darkness a ribbon of brilliant color erupted across the sky. It was brilliant reds and pinks that shimmered and danced across the sky.

"Oh," she gasped, surprised as it took her breath away.

"It's the northern lights," Ares exclaimed. "I've never seen them before."

"Never?" she asked.

He shook his head. "Nope. Spent my whole childhood in Toronto and most of my work is down south. Never got to see them. Too much light pollution."

"I love them. They're calming." Actually, she couldn't remember the last time she'd seen them. She really didn't pay attention to them anymore. Usually, they were faint and green, but these were strong and brilliant. She closed her eyes. "Maybe we can hear them."

"Hear them?" Ares questioned.

She nodded, keeping her eyes closed. "I've heard them hum. Once, when I was up in Yellowknife for work."

There was something about the lights tonight that grounded her and made her feel connected, brought her peace. Ares slipped an arm around her and pulled her into a side hug, like he always did. She rested her head against his shoulder and just stood there for a few moments, enjoying the lights.

Enjoying the moment.

Something she hadn't done in a long, long time.

CHAPTER SEVEN

IT HAD BEEN two weeks since they'd gone bowling and shared that moment on the turnoff of the highway with the northern lights. Pauly could have stayed there forever, wrapped up in Ares's arms, but Jeremy had woken up and it was getting late so they'd driven back to Canmore.

It had been a stolen moment, but it had been peaceful. There had been no other thoughts in her mind. It was empty and she'd felt grounded. Ares, in that moment, had completely centered her. It was more than just support and she couldn't let herself explore it further.

Pauly was trying not to think about it and instead just focus on the routine they were building both at work and with Jeremy.

Focusing on building that foundation for the year was a way to keep her mind completely occupied, or so she thought.

But it was the moments when they were at home, all together, that kept triggering those little thoughts. Dangerous thoughts, that made her want to think about Ares in a new light. Not just as a friend, but something more.

Thoughts she couldn't let herself entertain. She didn't want to ruin what they had, because she didn't want to lose someone else from her life and that was what she had to keep reminding herself of. The loneliness, the abandonment she kept locked away, seemed to be creeping out the more she thought about Ares. But it was a good reminder not to mess with what they had right now, because it worked. His presence made her feel not so alone anymore. Like she could be happy again.

Maybe life didn't have to be so hard.

Ares was getting along well with others at the station. Especially, the chief, who Pauly knew shared the love of mountain climbing. It was why Rex and Pierre had gotten along so well.

Still, anytime she turned her thoughts to Ares going up the mountain, into the most treacherous passes, she began to panic inside. The idea actually filled her with dread, which was silly because she'd used to love climbing. And it wasn't as though she could stop Ares from doing it. But every time she pictured him up there, all she could think about was him dying. Like Rex.

He's not Rex. But that thought didn't quell the anxiety. She wished she could tell him no.

But all he was, was her friend. She had no say over what he did.

There was a knock on her office door and

she glanced up to see Ares standing there. He looked so good in the dark navy uniform, with his shoulder-length hair tied back. For a moment, seeing him standing there, it was like no time had passed. She was transported back to when they were in college and working together. And how all the women who saw him in his uniform used to swoon.

"I don't know how you do it, Paul," Angela said, sighing.

"Do what?" Pauly asked.

"Work with that hunk," Angela stated. "That uniform looks so good on him. He's so dreamy."

Pauly glanced over at Ares and her cheeks heated. "He's handsome."

"Gorgeous," Angela corrected. "Is he single?"

"I think so."

"Isn't he your roommate?" Angela asked.

"Yeah, Rex and I room with him. I don't talk to Ares about his sex life though."

Ares looked at her and winked from across the classroom and she blushed again, but Angela was oblivious.

"He's cute." Angela sighed again.

"Ugh, stop objectifying my roommate and focus on the work," Pauly groaned. Although she couldn't blame Angela. Ares was very easy on the eyes.

"Hey," Ares said, waving a hand in front of your face. "You there? You zoned out."

"Yes," she cleared her throat. "Sorry. What's up?"

"My usual partner is out sick and there's a call about a trapped hiker on one of the trails. The hiker called in their coordinates and I have a track so we can follow the avalanche beacon. The hiker states they have a suspected sprained ankle and can't get out. Chief said we need to take the snowmobiles out and retrieve the hiker. The ambulance can't get to him where he is now, but we can bring him down to one of the junctions so they can pick him up."

Out on the mountain. Dread knotted in Pauly's stomach and she clenched her fists, digging her fingernails into her palms. She wanted to say no, but there was no one else. She had to do it, even though she was dreading it.

Just the thought of a beacon made her queasy, because she knew that sound well. She'd been in the office, listening to the sound of the beacons over the transceiver. The faint beating, almost like a heart rate monitor. Only Rex's heart had no longer been beating by the time they were able to track him.

Pull yourself together, Pauly.

"Sure. Let's go." She only hoped her voice didn't break as she said it.

It might do her some good to get some fresh air and get out there and work again. When she was with Ares on that trail for his training two weeks ago, it had been such a rush to be out in the field again. At first.

It was this or desk work, she told herself sternly. That wasn't what she'd been hired for, or what she'd thought she'd be doing as a paramedic. It was only fear holding her back.

They got their gear ready, everything they might need, including a portable stretcher that she and Ares might have to use to carry out the hiker, especially if the trail was too deep or too steep or too narrow for the snowmobiles, and had to go on foot with snowshoes or crampons.

That was something else that had been happening the last two weeks, so much snow. It was a deep layer of fluffy powder on top of hard-packed snow and ice, and it could look deceptively shallow.

Ares had managed to get his snowmobile safety registration; he was officially competent enough to ride his own machine. That meant they could take more gear and be extra safe.

As they headed out onto their access trail behind the station house, the snow was coming down in thick big fat fluffy flakes. The mountains weren't visible, but they could still see a good distance in front of them. They took their time, Pauly following Ares, who had the GPS coordinates mapped out on the navigation device.

The trail the hiker was on climbed up the mountain a bit and the snow got deeper. It was making Pauly more anxious. If they went up too much farther, there *could* be a threat of an avalanche, even though they weren't in an area that was prone to slide.

Her heart was pounding between her ears.

Don't have a panic attack, Pauly.

Ares came to a stop and she pulled up beside him.

"How much farther?" she asked, stiffly.

"Not much, just around that ridge. But I think we're going to have to take it on foot. It's so deep. I don't think the machines can get up there."

"Agreed."

They dismounted and collected their gear, strapping on their snowshoes and making their way along the trail. Even though it was still steadily snowing, Pauly could make out the trail that the hiker had taken. Every step farther up the mountain, her pulse quickened. It was like a dull roar, throbbing between her eardrums.

Breathe. You're safe.

It wasn't long before they saw the brightly colored snowsuit of the hiker in question One look at him, slumped over in the snow, made Pauly think that this injury was more than just a sprain. As they got closer, she could see he was partially buried in the snow. She could hear the familiar sound of a rescue beacon through the transceiver Ares held. It was a useful tool, one that was used by skiers when in the mountains, just on the off chance there was an avalanche and they were trapped.

Just hearing that familiar sound made her stomach knot.

Rex had a beacon. It was how they eventually found him, but in the end it had been too late. The beacon was to guide rescuers—it couldn't actually save a life.

"He's barely conscious," Ares remarked.

The man groaned. "Here. My name is… Chris."

"I'm Ares and this is Pauly—we're paramedics and rescue from Canmore. Thank you for being smart enough to provide coordinates," Ares said, sitting down next to the patient.

"I was walking and I misjudged the depth of the snow," Chris said, breathlessly. "Got my leg caught on a buried rock. There was a twist and a pop in my knee. Blinding pain. I can't feel it any longer."

Not feeling the extremity was not a good sign. Pauly exchanged a worried look with Ares. She took off her snowshoes to kneel down in the packed snow.

"It's not trapped anymore," she stated as she carefully removed the snow covering the leg. The moment she did so, she could see blood and bone poking through Chris's thin ski pants. "It's a fracture. We need a splint."

"My wife…" Chris said. "She'll be worried. And my kids."

"We'll call your wife as soon as we take care of you," Pauly stated.

"She's the one who called it in," Ares mentioned. "She had his last-known coordinates."

Pauly pursed her lips together. There was so much blood. The fracture looked worse than she'd initially thought as she gently palpated it, and she was starting to worry that Chris might have severed an artery. "We need a tourniquet."

Ares got one prepped and they placed it above Chris's knee. Chris slipped back into unconsciousness again as they splinted him.

"We have to get him to a hospital," Pauly murmured. "Fast."

What if they couldn't get him down quick enough? It was just the two of them.

"Agreed. We'll have to put him on the sled."

"I can carry the gear. No problem."

Working alongside Ares she managed to stabilize Chris and get him bundled up and secure on the small sled Ares had pulled up there. Ares was stronger so it made sense for him to pull it back down to the snowmobile.

Pauly took the bag that Ares had carried along with her own, and went ahead of them to try and pack down the trail even more so the sled could slide smoothly. It was a longer walk back down, because Ares was pulling Chris's weight, but they got him down without incident, and secured him on the bigger sled behind the snowmobile. Then they hurriedly packed their gear, called in to the ambulance about their meeting spot and Chris's status. Then, slowly, they began to head back down the trail.

Each step down to the snowmobiles had felt like an eternity, but the trip on the machines felt just as long. They had to get Chris to a hospital. All Pauly could think of was his poor wife and the agonizing torment she much be going through, wondering and waiting for word on her husband.

And she was a bit angry at Chris for coming up on this trail. Alone. It was a completely irrational anger, but it kept her focus sharp, helped her concentrate on getting him down to safety.

When they got to the junction, the ambulance was waiting there. Pauly filled Sean and Casey in on Chris's injuries, while Ares helped get him on the gurney. Once Chris was loaded, Sean and Casey drove the ambulance away and left the pair of them to take the machines back to the station.

"This feels slightly repetitive," Ares joked.

"Being left behind?"

He nodded. "Doing the hard work and letting Sean and Casey do the easy part."

Ares was only kidding—there wasn't anything easy about transferring a patient to the hospital. Sean and Casey could be stuck there for a while if the emergency room was busy. They wouldn't be able to leave their patient.

Pauly knew Chris would be a priority triage

with such a bad break and extensive bleeding, but all she could think about was his wife. She'd been in those shoes before.

"Well, it's almost five," Ares stated. "We better go."

She glanced at her watch. "Shoot. Yes, Jeremy will be waiting. We better get back to the station house, file our reports..." She trailed off as she tried to start her machine, but the engine wouldn't turn over. It just kept sputtering. Had she got snow in the system?

She pulled the starter cord again, but it was loose.

Great. Just great.

She let out a few choice cuss words. If she was late, Jeremy would worry.

"What's wrong?" Ares asked.

"I think I might've got snow in the exhaust," she muttered as she pulled off her gloves and opened the hood to take a look at the motor.

"Should we call someone?"

"No. I know how to deal with this."

Ares's eyes widened. "You do?"

"Why are you so shocked by that?" she questioned. "I think I should be highly offended by your surprise. I've changed multiple tires on the 401 in Toronto, during rush hour I might add, and I know how to put chains on my tires."

"Chains?"

Pauly huffed. "You need them to navigate mountain roads up here."

She took a deep breath, rubbing her temples. She had to concentrate, fix the problem so she could get home to Jeremy. And it was her responsibility to return the machines to the station.

Only, she couldn't get that sound of the beacon out of her head.

How worried she'd been listening to the beacons after the avalanche that had killed Rex. Listening to his particular beacon and hoping she'd see her husband again.

Focus.

"What can I do to help?"

"Grab me the tool box. It should have everything I need."

Ares handed her the tool box and she went to work. She pulled out the spark plugs and made sure there was no snow in the manifold, then sprayed some lubricant down into the holes. It was then she noticed the pull cord to start the engine wasn't working, so she pulled the plugs again and began slowly rotating the motor backward, until she had the right resistance on the pull cord.

Ares handed her tools as she needed. She was focused on the work, but she could sense it was growing darker. They either needed to get this fixed, or leave the machine there and call for a tow. She was about ready to do just that. All she could think about was getting home to Jeremy.

He'd be so worried, and she just wanted to let him know she was okay. He didn't even need to worry about her. She was *fine*. It was frustrating beyond belief.

"Blast this thing," she shouted, wanting to kick it.

"It's okay," Ares replied.

"No. It's not," she snapped, then she felt bad. "Sorry."

"No need to apologize. I get it."

She nodded. "We'll try this again."

"Deal."

"Okay," she replaced the plugs one more time. "Pull the cord for me now."

Ares pulled the cord, and the snowmobile revved to life.

Yes.

It was something Pauly had taught herself. She'd always been interested in how engines worked and liked to tinker. Rex knew nothing, but she didn't like being stuck anywhere. Sometimes, Rex had been a bit helpless. He always liked to joke how she took care of him. She was the adult. Something she was very used to.

Who takes care of me?

The thought caught her off guard, because she'd never even considered it before. Rex cared for her, but she'd always been more grounded than him. There had been times she wished she could be free, not be responsible for everything, but she wasn't even sure she knew what that was really like.

"That's impressive," Ares remarked.

"Thanks." She closed the hood and then packed up the tools. She wiped her hands and sat down on the seat for a moment, taking a breather. She was still shaking over the whole ordeal. Panic was still rising up in her, like the swell of a tide, even though the crisis had passed, and she didn't know how to control it. It was hard to breathe. All she needed right now was to be held, but she couldn't ask Ares to do that, so she wrapped her arms around herself, trying to get her nervous system to calm down and ground herself back into the present.

Ares stood in front of her and then knelt down. He reached out and touched her cheek, running the pad of his thumb across her skin. It felt good, comforting and she wanted a bit more. Only, she couldn't have more.

Could she?

"What're you doing?" she asked, her voice catching in her throat.

"You have a little smudge of something."

"Oh," she said, breathlessly. Her heart was racing. Then she placed her hand over his and closed her eyes, reveling in the warmth, the closeness. Even though she knew she shouldn't, she just wanted to hold on to this moment. This contact. This connection. It was calming.

"You okay?" he asked, moving closer.

She wanted to tell him no, she wasn't. She was lonely, she was numb and she just wanted to feel something—a tie to someone. She was also scared. Scared of the mountain, of leaving Jeremy. And then, the thought of almost losing Ares. Not that the hike had been risky, but what if she hadn't been here to help fix the snowmobile? What if he'd ended up trapped overnight and she hadn't known where he was?

It was all so overwhelming. All these feelings rushing through her. It was like she was spinning out of control today. What she needed was a moment of clarity through connection. Scooting forward she brushed a strand of Ares's hair away, running her fingers over his face as she leaned closer and pressed her lips against his.

It was only supposed to be a light kiss, but the moment their lips touched, a jolt of heat rushed through Pauly and the kiss deepened. She wanted more.

Ares wrapped his arms around her, pulling her flush against him. His tongue pushed past her lips and she melted against him, never wanting this rush, this flood of heat and desire to end. In his arms, she felt safe.

A crackle came over the radio. "Team 671 are you there, over?"

They both jumped back. Ares grabbed the radio. "Team 671 here."

"You're an hour late. You require assistance?" Erickson at the station house asked.

"Not required. Slight mechanical issue that's resolved. We'll be there shortly," Ares responded.

"Ten four." The radio went dead.

"What time is it?" Pauly asked.

"Six."

"Oh, my gosh. Jeremy will be super worried now. I lost track of time trying to fix the engine. I should've just called for a tow, but…my responsibility…" She was free-falling.

"It's fine, Pauly."

"No. It's not." She stood up. "About the kiss… I didn't mean to…"

"It's okay," he said, quickly.

"I hope this doesn't mean things will be weird."

Ares grinned. "No. Scout's honor."

Pauly nodded, but she was still kicking herself inwardly for letting her guard down, for falling for temptation. She could've ruined everything.

"Let's go." She put on her helmet.

The kiss had been amazing, but it was definitely a mistake she wasn't going to repeat again. She wouldn't ruin things. And she hated how she'd forgotten about everything else for a moment, including Jeremy. She was mad at herself for that.

They would be two hours late picking Jeremy up from the sitter and she had no doubt that he would be worried.

As much as she wanted to savour the kiss and

talk about what happened, this wasn't the time and the place for it. She had to get to Jeremy and let him know that she was okay.

They got back onto their snowmobiles and headed to the station house. As soon as Pauly got back she made a call to the sitter.

"Hi, Britt. It's Pauly."

"Hey, Pauly. You okay?"

"Yeah, we got stuck on a call," she replied. "Sorry I'm late."

"Oh, I don't mind. Do you want to talk to Jeremy?" Britt asked, quietly. Pauly could tell from her tone that Jeremy wasn't doing well. It made her heart sink. She just wished she could be beside him right now, to embrace him.

"Yes. Put him on."

"Hold on."

Paul could hear Britt calling for Jeremy.

"Mom?" Jeremy choked on the other end. She could tell he had been crying, which broke her heart even more.

"I'm here, Jere. I'm okay," she said, gently. "I'm really all right and I'll be home soon."

"You and Uncle Ari?" Jeremy's voice was still a bit wobbly.

"Yes."

"He's okay too?" Jeremy asked.

"We're both okay. We helped a man get to the hospital. A snowmobile broke down," Pauly explained. "I had to fix it."

She was trying to make light of it so Jeremy would cheer up.

"Oh, you fixed it?"

"Yep."

"Good," he said. "Are you coming to pick me up soon? I really want to see you."

"I am, with Uncle Ari. We'll be there as soon as we can, but don't worry, we're safe. I love you."

"Love you, Mom."

It was a hard phone call. It tore at Pauly's heart.

She couldn't do this anymore, field work, not until Jeremy was grown up. It wasn't fair to him.

She rushed through the motions to get the paperwork filed so they could leave and she could just hold Jeremy. She was still kicking herself for going out on the snowmobile in the first place.

"I have my report," Ares stated, walking into her office. "Just sent it to your inbox."

"Great," she answered, quickly logging back onto her email.

"Jeremy okay?" he asked.

"No. It's…it's the worry he's always had since Rex died. I haven't seen it in some time, since you came to stay with us. I guess I was foolish to think that he would be okay if I took more jobs out in the field." She dropped her head into her hands. This was not how she planned her life. There were a lot of things she was regretting right now.

Even the kiss.

Right now, she was regretting that too. Not

because it had been unwelcome—she'd wanted it badly—but she couldn't be selfish. She didn't have time to focus on pursuing anything romantic with anyone. Especially not with a friend, not with Ares. He wasn't even meant to be here for long.

She was going to ruin everything. She was going to make things awkward, be a burden to Ares. And he would leave, breaking Jeremy's heart even more.

And what about your heart?

She ignored that thought, because her heart didn't matter in all of this. Jeremy needed Ares, his uncle—what she needed didn't factor into this equation. She was fine.

Are you?

She had to hold tight to her decision. Ares was a wanderer. He'd be leaving in a year. She didn't need to complicate their lives further and push him away sooner.

Jeremy needed him.

What about you? that little voice insisted, but she ignored it. All that mattered was Jeremy and it was clear what her path was. She couldn't be heading out into the field, not with the uncertainty of it all. It would be too much for Jeremy.

Ares took a seat on the other side of her desk. "What're you thinking?"

"I'm thinking about taking a permanent administrative job. That way, Jeremy won't ever have to worry about me going out in the field again."

* * *

Ares's eyes widened. He couldn't really believe what he was hearing. Pauly sitting behind a desk, instead of doing what she loved? It didn't sit right, and he knew without a shadow of a doubt that she loved her career. He'd been there, right at the start. She loved her work.

"How can you think about walking away from your career?" he asked.

Her blue-gray eyes latched onto his and he knew instantly that he was treading on dangerous grounds. Pauly was stubborn and strong-willed.

"How could I not?" she asked. "I have to think about Jeremy."

"Jeremy will be fine," Ares stated, gently. "In time. Yes, he has trauma from what happened to his father and that's understandable, but you can't coddle him."

She sat up straighter, her eyes narrowed. "You don't know what you're talking about."

"I think I do," he replied. "Pauly, I know you want to protect him and if taking that desk job is how you think you can, then I can't stop you. But there are other ways accidents can happen. A desk job doesn't mean you're immune."

"It's the safer option."

"Is it?"

"It has regular hours."

"Yeah, and you know how many accidents happen just driving home from work?" The idea of her being hurt in a car crash filled him with horror, but he wanted her to see what she was saying made no sense. She was too good of a paramedic to give up so quickly.

Especially when she didn't *want* to give up.

She took a deep breath. "You're right. There are so many unknowns, but I know what's best for Jeremy."

"You can't sit around and wait for the bad to happen, because then you've wasted your life just sitting around and waiting. The best thing you can do for Jeremy is show him how strong you are and how you're not afraid to live out your dreams."

Pauly reached out and took his hand. "Thanks for always sticking by my side, but I know what's best."

He wanted to ask her if she really did, because to him it seemed like the wrong decision. Then again, he didn't have children, so maybe he was talking out of turn.

All he could do in this moment was support her, even though he thought what she was thinking about was a huge mistake. He'd just have to work hard and show her the job was worth it, even if it scared her. That it could work out.

"Of course, we promised. No weirdness between us, right?"

Although, he wanted just a little bit more of that weirdness. When they had shared that tender kiss up on the trail, it was like all his secret dreams were coming true. He'd been so shocked when she'd kissed him. The moment her soft luscious lips touched his, he was lost. His blood ignited, his senses reeled and all he wanted to do was drink in her sweetness.

In a way he was glad for the radio call from the station house, because he didn't want that kiss to escalate further. Well, part of him did. But he didn't want what they currently had to change.

He didn't want to lose what he had with Pauly.

There were a lot of estranged relationships in his life, and he wasn't going to risk letting this one with Pauly and Jeremy go, even if his heart wanted something completely different.

Pink tinged Pauly's cheeks and she took her hand back. "Right. No weirdness. Friends."

"Friends." The word was hard to say, it stuck thick in his throat, because that's not what he wanted. It just had to be that way.

"Okay, let's go get Jeremy and we'll have a cozy evening at home watching movies, or maybe playing some video games."

"That sounds like a plan." He stood and she came up to him and he pulled her close, hugging her like he always did, drinking in the scent of her, wanting so much more than just friendship.

Longing for another kiss, especially now.

But he'd made her a promise, one that he really didn't want to keep.

CHAPTER EIGHT

THIS WAS A side of Jeremy that Ares had never seen. He was almost unreasonable and just terrified. Back when he'd been out here that summer they spread Rex's ashes in the mountains, Jeremy had been withdrawn and grieving, but this anxious side of him was something new. It broke Ares's heart to see someone so young struggling so much, all because they had been a couple hours late.

Jeremy clung to Pauly when they picked him up. Pauly held on to him as they walked back to their house from the sitter's, just hugging him and stroking his back. Once they were home they made Jeremy's favorite food of hotdogs with macaroni, cheese and ketchup, which Ares did have a hard time stomaching, but it was all to cheer Jeremy up. He tried to make some jokes, but Jeremy wasn't interested.

Then they went to the couch and curled up on their big sectional, under fuzzy blankets. It took a while before Jeremy started to relax. Then he was begging to play video games with Uncle Ari and Ares was only happy to oblige.

After an hour of old-school gaming, Jeremy started yawning and fell asleep on the couch, exhausted. Ares just tucked him in and let him lie there.

"He's pretty good," Ares remarked as he got up. "I think I'm definitely too old and out of practice. My hand-eye coordination sucks."

"Same," Pauly mused, curled up in the corner and looking a bit worn-out herself.

It had been a long day. Ares still hadn't processed it all, including Pauly's admission she wanted to take a desk job. It was so not like her.

"Do you want some tea?" he asked.

"I would love some with honey in it."

"Done." He got up and put the kettle on.

"You got a package, by the way," Pauly said, offhandedly. "It's on the kitchen table there. It was delivered this morning."

Ares spun around and saw the box sitting there, wrapped in brown paper. Instantly, he recognized the writing. "It's from my mom."

"Well, open it. It might be some of her spanakopita."

"Uh, spanakopita wouldn't ship well. It's egg," he reminded her.

"Right. Oh, maybe it's her baklava. I could use some of that."

Ares chuckled. "You're probably right—it's probably treats."

Although, it had been some time since his mother had sent him anything. It was kind of out of the blue.

He undid the box. Pauly was right—it was several containers of his mother's baked treats. Pauly got up and scurried over to steal a piece of baklava as he poured the boiling water in the cups to let the tea steep. There was also a letter. Ares wasn't sure if he wanted to open it, but he'd have to eventually. There was no time like the present.

Dearest Ares,

I hope you are doing well in Canmore. I'm so glad you are there with your godson and Pauly. I like Pauly. You should settle down with her. I've called you a few times and got voicemail. Your father won't tell you, but the restaurant has closed and he has been diagnosed with pancreatic cancer. It's time you speak with him. I tried to get him to call, but you know your father. Stubborn. Please reach out, Ares, and visit soon.

Mom.

Ares's world dropped out beneath his feet.

Pancreatic cancer?

He was furious his father had forced his mother to tell him. His father was too hardheaded to call and tell him personally.

Would I even have picked up the phone if he called?

He cursed under his breath.

"What's wrong?" Pauly asked.

"My dad has cancer." The words seemed a bit dry as they came out of his mouth.

"Oh no," she said, quietly. "I'm so sorry. Do you have to head back to Toronto?"

"No." He folded the letter and put it in his pocket. "What's the point? He couldn't bother to tell me himself. He made my mom do it."

"You still haven't talked to your father since the divorce?" she asked.

"He didn't want to see me. Last time we talked I basically told him I didn't care if his family business failed. Well, the restaurant closed. I wasn't aware of that either until now."

Why couldn't his father tell him that? Although, what would Ares have really done about it? He hadn't wanted to run it, so he understood why he wasn't told. It stung all the same. He was angry at his father for divorcing his mother, for ending their happy family and for trying to put so much on his son's shoulders without ever seeing the value in what he did choose to do. But on the flip side Ares also missed him.

Deeply.

And now his dad was dying, and he was so angry at Ares for choosing his own path he hadn't even wanted to reach out.

If this was what family was all about, it was better that he remained single.

Is it?

When he looked at Pauly and Jeremy, he saw a different side. One he wouldn't mind being a part of.

"That is rough," Pauly agreed. "I had my own issues with my family, but it's better now. It got better."

"You had issues with your family?" he asked, curious. He hadn't realized that Pauly had any problems with her parents. The few times he'd met them, they'd seemed like nice, supportive people. He particularly liked her brother, Sam, who absolutely adored his big sister.

Most of all they were all still together. She had an intact family. He saw how they'd helped Pauly after Rex died. He saw the closeness and he'd often wondered how his family would react in that situation. Usually when he entertained those thoughts, it never turned out quite good.

"My family was never perfect when I was growing up," she sighed and fiddled with the string of the tea bag in her mug. "I grew up poor and I was left alone a lot taking care of Sam. I was about Jeremy's age when I accidentally turned on the stove and caused a fire. There was…we spent some time at my grandmother's house after that. There were some court cases and Sam and I were almost taken away. I almost caused the breakup of my family because I was supposed to know better."

Ares was floored. "You blame yourself for that? You were just a child."

"I had responsibilities. My parents worked and…"

"Again, you were just a child. You amaze me."

She looked shocked. "What do you mean?"

"You have your own amazing career, and still you've never been that kind of parent to Jeremy. I'm surprised you still talk to your parents."

She shrugged. "I'm working through it, but I guess I blame myself for it as much as you blame yourself for the distance with your father. The thing is, we talked as a family, we worked it all out. Maybe you should call your dad?"

Ares scrubbed a hand over his face. "I doubt he'd want to hear from me. My mother had to tell me everything. My father is very stubborn and set in his ways."

"Oh, really? I wonder who that's like." There was a little smile that played on her supple pink lips and a little twinkle in her eye as she teased him gently.

This was the kind of moment that made him want to take her in his arms. Their shared kiss played out in his mind again.

Teasing him.

Taunting him. The sweet taste of her was still burned on his lips, the softness of her body etched into his skin.

"I am not like my father," he grunted.

"I think you are. Just a bit. You're both very invested in your work."

"True." Ares couldn't argue with that logic. "I just don't know if he would want to hear from me."

Pauly blew across the top of her mug. "You'll never know unless you reach out."

"Why do you have to be so logical?" he asked, teasing slightly.

"Something you pick up when you're used to taking care of everyone for most of your life I suppose."

"And what about you?"

"What about me?"

"What about taking care of what you want?"

The question caught her off guard. She thought they were talking about Ares, and not her. She had her life figured out, for the most part.

Do you really?

The truth of the matter was, no she didn't. She just liked to think that she did. She'd had a clearer vision of what she wanted in life when Rex was still alive, but since his death, she wasn't sure where she was going.

She was free-falling and nervous about taking chances, like stepping down from the job she loved to work on the administrative side. And then there was that kiss, that connection she felt with Ares on the mountain. It had been so amazing to be held, to be intimate with someone again. Especially someone she trusted. She had initiated the kiss; she'd wanted it. In that moment she'd forgotten herself.

There was a part of her that could easily fall in love with Ares.

It could be so simple. She knew him; he loved Jeremy and Jeremy loved him. They were best friends and... Her thoughts trailed off because she just couldn't let herself think of Ares as more than just a friend.

I wouldn't be alone then.

Just that thought completely grounded her, because that was no basis to start a relationship with someone. She didn't want that insecurity to cloud her judgment, because she didn't want to hurt Ares and she didn't want to lose him.

Yet, she recalled the way she felt in his arms and the way his lips had fired her senses. She'd almost melted up there. It had been so long since she had that touch, that warmth. It made her feel alive again, when she'd been feeling numb for so long.

"I guess I do prioritize others first. I always have," she agreed.

"Exactly."

"I feel kind of embarrassed."

"Why?" he asked.

"I've never told anyone, except Rex, about what happened when I was kid. It was just easier to bury that side of myself."

"Thank you for sharing it with me. For what it's worth, you're the first I've told about my family too."

Her heart skipped a beat. "I guess that means we trust each other?"

"I suppose so." Ares came around the counter and stood in front of her; he reached out and touched her chin, tilting her head so she'd look at him. Her heart was beating so fast, her body reacting to the gentle touch of his strong hands.

What she wouldn't give to just let all her insecurities go and kiss him again and continue what they started. But the logical side of her brain was too loud. She couldn't give in, no matter how tempting Ares was.

She reached up and touched his hand. "Thanks for being my friend, Ares. Jeremy and I would be so lost without you."

"Anything for you…for you both." His voice was deep, husky and it made her body ache with need. He was so close. What harm would it do to just give in, for one night?

"Mom?" Jeremy called from the couch, groggy. As much as she didn't want to break this connection with Ares, she was glad for it.

Ares stepped back and Pauly headed over to the couch where Jeremy was rubbing his eyes.

"Right here, buddy," Pauly answered. "You fell asleep on the couch. You ready for bed?"

"Yep."

"I'll carry him," Ares offered.

And before she could argue Ares had scooped up Jeremy in his arms. Jeremy curled up against Ares and rested his head on his shoulder. Her heart melted watching him carry her son up the stairs. A sob welled up in her throat and tears stung her eyes as she bit back the rush of emotion.

Jeremy needed Ares in his life and there was no way she could let her own emotions jeopardize that. She didn't want to ruin things by driving Ares away.

They needed him.

Ares tossed and turned most of the night. He was going over the kiss, the conversation with Pauly over her giving up work in the field, but also Jeremy's reaction when they picked him up. Seeing his godson suffer tugged at the fibers of his soul. He understood now why Pauly thought going to a desk job would be better. He still didn't agree, but he sympathized.

Pauly was doing all she could to shield Jeremy from pain. It was admirable, but Jeremy was old enough to understand more than she realised. What he needed was a man-to-man talk. And who better to give him that than his godfather?

So Ares made sure he was up bright and early, hoping Jeremy came down first. He did, looking tired, like he hadn't slept much. It hurt to see a kid struggling so much at such a young age.

"Morning, buddy," Ares greeted.

"Can I have cereal?" Jeremy asked, sullenly. He was completely not his usual happy-go-lucky self. It reminded Ares of the sad, heartbroken boy from a couple years ago.

"Sure. It's Saturday. I'll have some too. I would ask you if you slept okay, but it looks like you were wrestling gators all night."

A minuscule smile crept on Jeremy's face. "No gators in Canmore."

"Probably it's too cold."

Jeremy nodded. "Yeah."

"You okay?" It was a silly question. Ares knew he wasn't, but he didn't want to bombard Jeremy right away.

Jeremy climbed up on a stool, rubbing his eyes. "I was scared yesterday."

"I know," Ares replied, calmly, as he pulled cereal out of the pantry cupboard. "But you don't have to be scared whenever your mom is late. It's not always a bad sign. My parents were late all the time, working, and they were fine."

Jeremy sighed. "Yeah, I can't help it though."

"I get it, pal, I know it's hard. But what happened to your dad… That was an unusual accident. It doesn't happen often. And, remember, your mom can handle a lot. She's awesome."

"Yeah, I guess…"

"I mean, she saves lives. Like at the bowling alley. You remember that, right?" Ares asked, softly, glad Jeremy was opening up instead of shutting down.

Jeremy looked at him in disbelief. "Of course."

"Yesterday, she did the same."

Jeremy rested his head against his fist. "She did?"

Ares nodded. "We were out helping a man who'd gotten hurt on the trail. She saved his life. He had kids. Like you."

Jeremy didn't say much, just nodded, but then looked up. "So why was she late?"

"Snowmobile problems. Remember? We weren't in any danger, except of getting cold. And not for long. It's pretty neat that your mom can fix them, huh?"

Jeremy smiled. "Yeah."

"Your mom loves her job, but not as much as she loves you. She's good at it, but she might give it up."

"Why?"

"She doesn't want you to worry, pal. Neither do I." Ares felt a lump in his throat. He loved Jeremy so much. It killed him to see him suffering. "But maybe you don't have to worry quite so much. What do you think?"

Jeremy looked thoughtful. "I don't want her to quit. It's cool what she does. Maybe… I think I can be brave."

"I know you can." Ares tousled his hair. "I'm

glad you think your mom is cool. Guess that means you think *I'm* cool too, huh?"

Jeremy smiled, just a little. "Of course. You're the coolest. You save lives too. Just like Mom."

It made Ares's chest tight with emotion to see that hint of a smile back on his face. And even though he'd been the one to say the words first, hearing them reflected back to him in Jeremy's sincere voice made him glow with pride. "Wish everyone saw it that way, buddy."

Jeremy looked confused. "Who wouldn't?"

Ares sighed. "My dad," he said, thinking again of the letter, all the feelings it had stirred up. He pushed the thoughts away. "That's not the point."

"Well, that's silly." Jeremy's nose was wrinkled. "Maybe he just worries like I worry."

"Maybe." Ares didn't want to take the conversation down that road, not when Jeremy was finally looking happier. "But, hey, I might not be a mechanical genius like your mom, but I can look after myself too. Did you know I climbed Everest?"

Jeremy's eyes widened. "You did? Weren't you scared?"

"A bit. It's the tallest in the world and a dangerous climb, but I'm here still. Sometimes, you just have to decide to experience something amazing. You can't let worry and fear control your life."

Jeremy nodded. "Mom used to climb mountains with Dad. I saw pictures. Wonder why she stopped?"

Ares was pretty sure he knew why. "I wonder about that too. You know, she worries about you a lot too."

"She doesn't need to. I can be brave for her."

"You sure can," Ares said, proudly pouring him cereal.

Jeremy was clearly still thinking as he poured in the milk. "She's good at taking care of people. Like the bowling alley guy."

"Exactly. Sometimes, she'll get delayed. You've got to be brave for her and only think of how she's safe, because she's trained."

"Yeah, you're right. I do." Jeremy took a bite of cereal. "She's a cool mom. She needs to do her work. Help others."

"Most definitely," Ares agreed.

"I'll be brave."

"I know, buddy. You'll worry, I get that, but you're strong. Like your mom. And like your dad. You know, he wanted to climb Everest too? He would've gone to the top with me."

"Why didn't he?"

Ares grinned and poked Jeremy's nose. "He was here. You were born that same day."

Jeremy laughed. "I think I can be strong for Mom. I'll make her proud."

"Of course you will, buddy. You're an awesome dude."

Jeremy was his bubbly self again, and Ares could see the pride in his face. Admiration for his mom and some for Ares too. That felt surprisingly good.

Maybe Jeremy was right, and his dad did worry about him. Ares wanted to believe that, but it was hard to ignore years of frosty silence.

Still, it got him thinking about things he never thought before. About family. He remembered what Pauly had told him last night. He'd been running from something he thought could never work because of his own parents, but she'd had a rough childhood too. She hadn't run from marriage or a child—she'd embraced it. And made it work.

Maybe he didn't have to be so scared about settling down. He was trying to convince Pauly not to give up on something good because of fear. Maybe he should learn to take his own advice?

There was something to be said for Saturday morning cereal talks.

CHAPTER NINE

AFTER HE AND Pauly had shared that moment over tea a week ago, Ares had thought something more might've happened. But nothing much had changed. Except, his talk with Jeremy had gone well, and that pleased him. Everything else just sort of went back to normal, even though it didn't feel normal.

It had felt like a huge burden had been lifted off his shoulders when he told her about his estrangement from his father. It had always been this secret shame he carried around with him. Basically, he was unloved. Talking with Pauly that night was the first time he'd really opened up about his family and what had happened between them, since telling her about the divorce so long ago in college. No one in his family ever talked about it; they always put on a brave face. It was a shameful failure, not to be discussed.

It was almost like his parents were trying to hide it or something, which was silly given how his father moved out. But his father liked perfection. Ares could see that now. Successful business, children who had admirable careers.

Except Ares.

Since college, Ares had kept it all locked inside too, eating away at him. All these years he'd been living his life in defiance of his father's disappointment, thinking that he was out of his control, but maybe in a way his dad had been influencing his choices after all.

Either way, it had been good to finally share that truth with someone.

And now that Pauly had opened up about her childhood, about her fears, he understood her better. He was touched she'd felt so comfortable sharing that vulnerability.

He'd never felt as connected to anyone as he did in that moment. He'd thought he really knew Pauly, but he hadn't known this side of her. So she'd been hiding something secret away all these years too, and the fact that he was the first person she'd shared it with meant so much. Neither of them was alone. Their friendship had become deeper than he'd thought possible.

Except, now he wanted more.

I can't have more.

Something it was getting harder and harder to convince himself of as he spent more time with Pauly and Jeremy. Even though he lived his life on his terms and the way he wanted, nothing had ever compared to the last few weeks in Canmore. This was exactly what family should be.

Yet, this was temporary, because there was an end date. His contract here was only for a year.

He'd have to move on next fall.

Who says?

The idea of leaving his work, his traveling to take this job here permanently was terrifying. It was something he never contemplated before.

"Hey, Galanis, there's a meeting with the chief in boardroom three," Erikson said sticking his head into the locker room where Ares had just finished putting his stuff away.

"Thanks," Ares acknowledged, waving to him.

He had to put everything out of his mind and concentrate on work. Usually when thoughts were plaguing him all he had to do was just focus on the job and it would be easy to clear his mind. The problem now was the main thing he was ruminating on was Pauly and he couldn't escape that.

She was everywhere.

Ares found boardroom three easily enough. Everyone was taking seats. Pauly was at the front and he sat down next to her.

"Any idea what this is about?" he whispered.

"No idea," Pauly responded. "I wonder if he's going to address the influx of snow we've been having steadily since the end of October? It's a bit early for this amount, so they might be closing some of the trails and passes."

"That would make sense." Ares sat back and crossed his arms. "But would that require a meeting?"

"It could. We'd have to go over protocol on rescues. Some of those trails and passes are treacherous."

The chief, Pierre Lloyd came into the room and took to the podium at the front.

"Good morning, everyone," Lloyd addressed the crowd.

There was a murmur of "morning" returned.

"I've called you all here because we're getting reports of serious avalanches."

The moment the chief mentioned the word *avalanche* Pauly's spine straightened and Ares saw her hands ball up into tight fists. He wanted to reach out and comfort her, but he knew she'd hate that.

Chief Lloyd continued. "I've been conferring with the station houses in Banff, Kananaskis about the amount of snow and the temperature. Environment Canada has also confirmed with us about the extreme fluctuations. With the up and down temperatures there have been a lot of avalanches, more than we usually get for this time of year. Highway 93 headed north from Banff to Jasper has been closed. Also with this amount of snow, the influx of tourists and skiers has increased exponentially. And with the increase in tourists, signs of closed trails and dangerous ski hills are often ignored. We all know Russ is once again operating that foolish helicopter ride where skiers are dropped and then ski down; and with the way the snow packs are, it's a great danger. What I need is rescuers who are skilled mountain climbers to join a joint rescue team, that, when called, will traverse in the high mountain passes to perform rescue operations of possible trapped people."

There were a few questions and Ares leaned over to Pauly.

"Russ does what?" Ares asked, under his breath.

Pauly rolled her eyes and nodded. "I don't think it's smart, but Russ is a licensed pilot and the ski-ers do have insurance and take classes. They like the extreme ski from high in the mountains."

"I guess I can't really complain… I climb them, they just hurtle themselves down them?" He was trying to make light of it, because he could sense Pauly was anxious and he wanted to diffuse the situation.

Pauly sniggered. "Yeah, you could put it like that."

"Any more questions? And not about Russ and his black diamond helicopter rides," Lloyd asked, with a tone of weariness.

There were a few laughs in the crowd.

Ares put up his hand. "I have mountain climb-ing experience. I would like to volunteer."

The moment the words came out of his mouth

he heard Pauly's head whoosh to look at him and he could feel her eyes boring into the side of his face. But she shouldn't be surprised that he was volunteering. Part of the reason he took this job in Canmore for the year was because he had mountain climbing skills. He might as well put them to work. He knew she would be worried and he felt bad, but he was experienced and they needed him.

He'd climbed Everest and some of the other biggest peaks in the world. This is what he wanted to do.

"I was hoping you would step up, Galanis," Lloyd stated, smiling. "Just need you to sign these forms and then we're going to join in on a virtual meeting with the other station houses and go over protocols this afternoon."

Ares nodded and got up to sign the forms with Lloyd. He glanced back once, but Pauly was no longer staring at him. She was staring down at her hands and looked upset. He felt bad, but this was what he loved to do.

And this is why you can't be tied down, a little thought reminded him.

Only, he wasn't sure if that was really the problem. He knew that Pauly was thinking about Rex and about how he died, but Rex had died doing what he loved and saving lives. That's what Ares was here for. If saving lives didn't matter to him, he would've never become a paramedic. He would've done just what his father wanted and taken over the family restaurant.

And been completely miserable.

As much as it pained him to turn his back on Pauly and leave that room with the chief, this was his career. He had the skills and he needed to be there to help.

Pauly didn't see Ares for the rest of the day and she wasn't surprised by that. He was going through some training about the protocols for avalanches and rescue operations on high mountain passes. Meanwhile, she went out on a few local calls with Erickson, in the ambulance.

Though she tried to completely focus on her work, she couldn't help but think about Ares up there on the mountains and the danger he was putting his life in.

It made her sick to her stomach when she thought about it. All the anxiety possible poured through her over the thought of something happening to him. She cared for Ares, and it terrified her to think of losing him.

Every possible worst-case scenario ran through her mind and she tried to strategize a solution. Only she couldn't. All she could come up with was fear, fear of something she couldn't control.

I'm only thinking like that because of what happened to Rex.

Which was completely true.

When Rex had been out on the perilous mountains, she'd been a bit concerned, but she'd never really worried about it, not until he died on the job and left her alone. It was then that she'd become angry at herself for not stopping him from taking those dangerous rescue operations. Logically, she knew he'd died doing what he loved, saving others, but she was still angry he'd left her.

Now the thought of losing Ares up there as well? It was too much for her to handle. Her heart couldn't survive that.

Her stomach twisted and a stress headache was starting to pound behind her eyes.

This is why he agreed to come and work with fire and rescue services. He wanted to be out on the mountain.

In theory it had all sounded good, but now faced with reality, she wasn't handling it very well. It wasn't like she had a real say over the jobs he took either. She wasn't his significant other, she was just his friend.

That thought cut her to the quick, because there was a part of her that wanted to be more than just a friend. A part she was trying hard to ignore.

But she was finding herself entertaining the idea of more with him and that was a scary prospect indeed, because she knew how he felt about marriage and what a transient life he led. Would he really want to be tied down in Canmore to a widow with a young child? That wasn't just a step to settling down, that was *really* settling down. And if things didn't work out, then Jeremy would lose his beloved Uncle Ari and she'd lose her best friend.

It just wasn't worth the risk, no matter what her heart was telling her in this moment.

As she finished up her final report and sent it off, Ares came back into the station house and looked a bit exhausted as he approached her, his knapsack over his shoulder.

"Hey," she greeted, trying to sound all bubbly and cheery instead of letting her voice shake with the existential dread that was screaming deep inside her. "How was your day?"

"Long, but I'm excited about being part of the team." There was a twinkle in his eyes as he started to tell her about everything that happened during the day. She could see the fire and passion in his face and hear it in his voice. All the while her leg began to bounce with nervousness. She had to place a hand on her knee to stop it.

There was no way she could ask him to not do it. She didn't have that right.

"I'm glad." Which was a complete lie.

He cocked an eyebrow and stared down at her. "Uh-huh. Sure."

"What?" she asked.

"I know this is hard."

She shook her head vehemently. "It's fine. This is what you came to Canmore to do. You brought your own equipment here, for heaven's sake. I get it, Ares. Am I worried? Sure, but I know that you're a skilled climber."

Although, Rex had been a skilled climber too. Didn't matter how good or careful you were, Mother Nature was always more powerful in the end.

His eyes narrowed and he looked at her uncertainly, like he didn't quite believe her. "I don't think it's fine."

She let out a long sigh. "I guess there's no hiding it."

"No." He ran his hands through his hair. "It'll be okay, Pauly."

"You can't be certain of that," she snapped.

"No. I know I can't." He frowned. "I have to do it though."

Pauly felt guilt for making him feel this way. That was not her intention. "Look, I'll worry, but I swear I'll be fine, Ares."

Ares didn't look convinced. He let out a sigh. "We should do something fun tonight. It's Friday and it's snowing… Maybe tonight is the night we take Jeremy tobogganing?"

"You say that with such enthusiasm," she teased, forcing herself to lighten up.

"I promised him, and I liked it as a kid. I'm just tired."

"You don't have to do it."

He groaned and then grinned. "I know, but it'll

take your mind off everything right? You can't really think when you're freezing cold and throwing yourself down an icy hill on a piece of plastic."

Pauly laughed. "No. I suppose not, but you have a shift tomorrow. Are you sure you want to do this?"

He waffled. "No, but let's do it anyway."

"Okay." Pauly was still concerned, but her anxiety was melting away as she tried to focus on how happy Jeremy would be tonight. "You know, I was hoping you'd put up more of a fight about sledding."

His laugh was loud and joyous, like his old self. "Yeah, I know. I'm surprised at myself."

"You'll forever be Jeremy's favorite uncle."

"Good. You almost ready to go?"

"Yep. All done."

"Let's go then." Ares held out his hand and she took it. It felt so right to slip her hand in his and she did feel slightly better, but she was going to continue to fret about it. She couldn't help it.

She was waiting for the unknown and that was never a good thing.

Why did I suggest this?

This was the question that Ares kept asking himself every time he got to the bottom of the steep sledding hill and had to climb his way back up. Pauly was right. Definitely a different experience as an adult versus being a kid. Especially after a long work day.

He had to admit it was kind of fun to toboggan in the dark though. The sledding hill was lit up and there were big fat flakes falling. When you got to the top of the hill you could see the town of Canmore's lights twinkling. It was the middle of November and people were starting to put up their holiday lights in preparation for Christmas. With the snow and the colorful lights it was cozy. In the daylight, it looked like a cute mountain village, which it was. At night, with this weather and at this time of year it was almost magical.

Rocketing down the hill was a blast, even though the snow stung his face as he slid, but the hard part came at the bottom, when he had to get off the sled with Jeremy and climb back up the hill in his snow gear. After a long day of just sitting and going through rescue and emergency protocols, his body was stiff and the climb got a little tedious.

"Come on, slow poke," Pauly teased as she grabbed the toboggan from him and raced up the hill after Jeremy. Ares grumbled and trudged after them.

He may have grown up in Canada, but he really didn't like the cold and snow. Unless he was climbing a mountain, and even then it was hit or miss. When he'd been up on Everest it had been so cold and snowy, but the difference there was the warmth that came from the accomplishment.

An accomplishment I celebrated alone.

No one had been with him on that climb. When he'd called his mother on his satellite phone from the summit, all she had said to him was, *"That's nice."*

His father didn't even know about it.

That summit, that climb, had made him realize how utterly alone he was, but that was the life he'd chosen for himself.

Now, spending time here on this ridiculous hill, in the snow, hurtling himself down on a sled, he wondered again if he was making the right decisions in his life. Maybe, just maybe, he didn't want to be alone after all?

But his work was perilous. Traveling to some countries was dangerous and now mountain rescue… He was always going to be putting his life on the line. How could he even think about putting Pauly and Jeremy in that situation, afraid of losing someone, again? Would she want to open her heart to another dare devil?

Ares seriously doubted it. The last thing he ever wanted to do was hurt her. And it was clear she was already struggling with it all.

"Let's all go down together," Jeremy shouted, his eyes sparkling in the dark and his cheeks bright red. "On the same sled."

"Can we all fit?" Ares asked, puzzled.

"Sure we can," Pauly said. "Jeremy in the front, then me and then you and you can push us off."

Jeremy got into the front of the sled and then Pauly sat behind her son, her legs straddling him. Ares's pulse began to race as he thought about coming up behind Pauly, once again, just like on the snowmobile that first day of training.

Get a grip on yourself.

He slid up behind her, her body pressed against his chest. His legs were so long that, stretched out, they went down the length of the toboggan.

"Let's go!" Jeremy squealed, holding the rope at the front of the curled sled.

"Okay, hold on." Ares used his hands to push off and then wrapped his arms around Pauly as they shot down the steep incline. Jeremy was shouting and so was Pauly. Ares just reveled in having Pauly in his arms and spending time with her and Jeremy.

It was like a picture-perfect moment of domesticity.

And he loved it.

Every second of it, even in the cold.

As they came to the bottom of the hill, he let go of Pauly's waist and slowed their descent so they didn't take out one of the dozen other people at the bottom of the hill. A fast-moving sled could knock someone straight into the air.

"That was so much fun!" Jeremy shouted.

"It was," Pauly agreed breathlessly. "How about

we go and get some hot chocolate now at the coffee shop?"

"And a donut?" Jeremy asked, excitedly.

"Sure," Pauly agreed. "I'd usually say no to sugar, but you're already pretty hyper from all this sledding."

Ares stood up and stretched. "Hot chocolate and donuts sound great, but after that will have to hit the hay early tonight. I have work tomorrow."

Jeremy paused. "Don't you work with Mom?"

"Sometimes," Ares said, picking up the sled. "And sometimes our shifts will be different."

Jeremy nodded, but went a little quiet. "You'll be okay though, right? We were going to play video games tomorrow night."

Ares put his arm around his godson, pulling him into a reassuring side hug. It wasn't like he could promise him that nothing would happen, but he didn't want Jeremy to worry either. "Remember about Everest."

Jeremy nodded. "Right!"

"I'll be back to whip your butt at that racing game," Ares teased.

"Cool." Jeremy broke away and ran toward the truck.

Pauly was worrying her bottom lip. "I'm sorry about that."

"It's okay. He needs to heal just as much as you."

"What did you mean about Everest?" she asked.

"I told him about doing that climb. The one Rex and I planned to do together until *someone* got pregnant."

Pauly laughed. "It wasn't all my fault."

"I know, but Jeremy was pretty impressed."

"No doubt! Thanks for being his pal."

"I'll always be that," Ares stated.

She nodded and he pulled her into a quick hug with his free arm. She wrapped her arms around him and it felt so good to have her snuggled against him, even with all the layers. He could stay like this forever.

He could be with both of them forever. He wanted to tell Pauly how much he loved her. Only he couldn't form the words. He couldn't be selfish.

Instead, she pulled away.

"Hot chocolate is on me," she said.

"Deal."

CHAPTER TEN

"THERE'S A BAD snowstorm coming. I can see it brewing on the horizon," Pauly remarked on Tuesday, when she came back to work. She'd been off for the last couple of days, but now they were back on the same shift.

Ares had been working solidly. His next day off was on Thursday. He'd kind of missed working alongside Pauly, but partnering with Erikson the last few days hadn't been so bad. Even though he saw her at night, when he was on the job, he could finally put some distance between them. At least that was his theory.

Honestly, he'd *tried* to throw himself into his work to forget about her, but he couldn't. All he could think about was being together on the sledding hill, all the tender moments they shared and how much he was enjoying this life, pretending to be a family. He thought he would miss his work traveling to different exotic locations, but he didn't.

In Canmore he felt a bit more grounded, like it could be home for him too.

"I saw there was a bad storm. They're even calling it a blizzard," he said. He sat down at her desk, trying to ignore all the possibilities raging in his mind. "Think we'll get a lot of calls?"

It was a joke—he knew they would—but she gave him some serious side-eye. "Of course we will. It's going to be a busy day and night."

"Is Jeremy at the sitters?" Ares asked.

She nodded. "Britt knows I might be late. It's happened before in the past, when Rex and I both worked long hours during a storm or even forest fires. Jeremy loves her boys, so he's in good hands. He's not alone, so that's the main thing."

"And how did Jeremy take it?" Ares asked, curious.

"Well, actually," Pauly admitted. "He took the news well. I'm glad."

Ares could sense the hesitation in her voice as she said those words and now he understood that trepidation a bit better. The pain of feeling abandoned. He understood that, as well.

"You never wanted to move back to Toronto?" he asked.

"No." She smiled. "I do love it here. I have friends here."

"Yes, but more family out there. More help."

"I get that. Rex's family have been trying to talk me into moving back forever, but this is where I made my life with Rex and he's up there in the mountains. I don't want to leave him there. I want to stay here."

"I get that."

"Do you? You don't seem to want to settle."

"I like exploring..." he trailed off, because he really didn't want to admit right now that he'd been thinking a lot lately about maybe planting his own roots. It felt too scary an endeavor to even admit. There was all the uncertainty.

All the unknowns.

As he was sitting there pondering, not filling out some crucial paperwork he needed to fill out, the small office where Pauly worked became darker. The room had huge glass windows overlooking Canmore, and it was as though night was creeping up on them outside. It was only ten in the morning. Then there was a blast of wind, howling and whistling fiercely.

It startled Pauly and she looked up from her computer, staring out the window. "Wow."

Ares followed the direction of her gaze. He couldn't see Canmore, except for some streetlights barely shining through the snow. There was a loud rumble, and he knew it was the wind hitting the side of the station house. He'd never seen anything like this before. Toronto rarely got such intense weather—all the tall buildings downtown acted like a natural windbreak. He'd never really experienced a true whiteout.

This was like something out of a movie.

He got up and wandered to the window. "This is wild."

"This is definitely intense. I mean, Canmore gets snow, it's why people come here to ski in the Rockies, but since I've been living here I've never seen an actual blizzard."

An alarm went off. An emergency call.

There was no more time to talk about it. Now was the time to get to work and save lives.

When he'd started his shift, Ares had had a feeling in the pit of his stomach that this was going to be a long, gruelling day, and it looked like he was being proven right.

There was really no pause as they attended call after call. There were accidents on the highway, because the snow was causing whiteout conditions. It wasn't long before the RCMP put up barricades and started shutting down roads to motorists. The snow was falling so rapidly that snowplows were trying to keep the roads clear, just so that emergency services could still get through. The wind was blowing the fresh powder that accumulated across every open area. Cars were being buried, making the snowplows work even harder as they had to stop and tow out people who'd been stranded.

The hospital was becoming overloaded with patients in the ER and it was only three in the afternoon. Ares and Pauly were finishing a drop-off there when they got another call.

"Calling 671," the switchboard operator said. "We have reports of a stranded hiker on Spruce Ridge Pass. Please respond."

"Copy that. We're on our way," Pauly responded as she carefully pulled out on the snow-covered roads. As they made their way to the hiking trail, it wasn't so much the snow that was hard, but the ice hidden under the layers of powder. The drive became more and more treacherous, especially as they drove a little bit out of town to where some of the steeper trails were.

The ambulance was equipped with chains on the tires for situations like this.

"Who would hike in a blizzard?" Ares asked as Pauly navigated the winding road to the parking lot at the head of the Spruce Ridge Pass trail.

"Lots of people. This trail is usually shut for winter, though," she said, through gritted teeth. And he knew she was struggling with her fear of going up the mountain again. "It's a summer trail for backcountry camping. But we get the odd daredevil who ignores the signs and goes out on the trails in the winter anyway."

Ares saw the flashing lights and flares of the RCMP in the parking lot. Not only was it dark from the onslaught of snow and howling winds, but night was coming. Daylight Savings Time had passed, so darkness came earlier and would continue to come earlier until they reached the winter solstice in December, a month away.

They got out of the ambulance and began to pack the gear they'd need.

The RCMP constable came over to them. "Glad you could make it. I'm Constable Greer. My team have located the hiker, but we're having a hard time traveling down the slope. I heard one of you was adept at climbing?"

"I am," Ares stated. He grabbed the gear bag that had all the equipment needed for a mountain rescue. The trail was higher in elevation than the town of Canmore, but he wouldn't really call this "up the mountain." Still, Constable Greer had mentioned that the injured hiker had slipped down a slope, and they wouldn't have the equipment to attempt a rescue. And because of the weather, they couldn't airlift the hiker out. He'd need to be carried.

"Great," Constable Greer stated. "The hiker is injured, fairly bad."

"Lead the way, Constable." There was a definite nervous edge to Pauly's voice. Ares wished that he could comfort her and tell her it was going to be okay, but this wasn't the time or place for that. As they were heading up the trail another paramedic team joined them, which he was glad for.

Ares was the only one with experience climbing mountains and scaling cliffs, so it became

quickly apparent that he would be the one leading this rescue. He'd done rescues on cliffs before, just not in the snow. They packed as much
emergency gear as they could. Their packs were
big. At least with a large team they would be able
to carry the rescue toboggan together, as well as
the litter. It would be sent down a guideline, then
the patient would be strapped down and lifted off
the side of the cliff.

All Ares could think about was the sled they
had used with Jeremy a few days ago, the happiness he had felt going down that hill.

This bright orange rescue toboggan was a bit
more sophisticated than Jeremy's sled. They'd be
able to secure the litter carrying the trapped hiker
inside and transport him out. It even had handles
to allow them to pull or push the toboggan down
the trail.

It was at least a twenty-minute hike to the site
of the accident, a narrow trail leading to a steep
drop-off. There were markers to indicate the
slope, but it was hard to see in the snow. It hadn't
been a smart idea on the part of the hiker, taking a mountain trail in a blizzard, but that was an
opinion Ares would keep to himself and let the
RCMP figure it all out after.

All he had to do was rescue the trapped man.

At least the blizzard was dying down for now,
but the darkness was coming in quickly. Pairs

were tethered together to keep each other safe, just on the off chance of an avalanche.

Ares hoped that didn't happen, but it was better to be safe than sorry in this kind of situation. Pauly was tied to him, so he was able to keep his eye on her.

Constable Greer, who was leading the pack, put up his arm. "Here!"

Ares and Pauly made their way to the side. He unhooked Pauly in case he slid down the slope and because he needed to be able to move to get in his harness.

Flares were set so he could see where the hiker had fallen. He was against a tree that jutted out the side of the rock face. Underneath was a hundred foot drop to the forest below.

The rest of the slope had a gentle incline down. Of course the unfortunate hiker had to fall in the one spot that was steep.

Ares was working to calculate his artificial high direction so that he could tell the team where to anchor the guidelines in order to allow the litter the smoothest transition back up the side of the cliff.

"Tell me what to do," Pauly said.

He could hear the fear in his voice, and he could see it in the way her lips were pressed together in a tight line. But he admired her dedication and commitment to the work. She was willing to swallow her trepidation down. Which was good, because he needed her right now. He needed his partner, someone he trusted, to do this risky rescue.

Ares hoped, if they succeeded here, she'd change her mind about giving up her career to sit behind a desk.

As he got hooked into his harness and put on the rest of his safety gear, he instructed the rescuers. "We need to anchor the tracking line system here and here."

Once everything was secure, he started his descent, gently rappelling on the cliff, trying not to stir up too much snow. It was hard going; the storm had begun to intensify again.

There was a creak. Ares's first thought was *avalanche*. But nothing shifted.

Once he had made it to the hiker, Ares saw he was unconscious, just like the skier from the riverbank. He could tell that the man's arm was dislocated or possibly fractured because it was at an odd angle. There was also a definite contusion on his head and some bleeding, but it was hard to see more than that in the dark, even using the headlamp on his helmet.

"Send down the rescue litter," he called up.

"Okay," Pauly shouted.

Ares waited as the litter was lowered and grabbed it. Then he focused on getting the injured hiker safely strapped on. Once he had everything secure, he gave a tug on the guideline. "Pull him up!"

The litter began to rise and Ares followed, climbing slowly beside it and making sure that it didn't get bumped or jostled or caught in a tree branch. Finally, it disappeared over the top of the cliff, and Ares climbed after it. He got unhooked, then they loaded the patient onto the toboggan.

"Head contusion, left pupil dilated. Possible fracture or dislocation of the left arm," Ares informed the other paramedics.

The four of them worked together to secure the man. Then the two other paramedics headed straight back down the trail, pulling the rescue toboggan. Pauly hooked herself back up to Ares and they packed up the gear.

There was a crack, and they all stopped to listen.

"We better get down off this trail," Constable Greer stated.

"We're good to go," Pauly said, but Ares could hear the gut-wrenching fear in her voice.

He knew she was thinking what he was thinking. It had been snowing steadily for hours and there was at least thirty centimeters in the pack above them.

Greer and his officers led the way, Pauly just behind them. They took their time, carefully making their way down. But then there was a large snap and a *wumpf* sound.

"Avalanche!" Greer shouted from up ahead.

The snow was going to cut them off from the RCMP. It was headed straight for him and Pauly.

"Swim, Pauly," Ares shouted over the roar. "Swim to the side, back toward me."

Don't let me lose her.

It was his last thought as the snow poured like a river from above them.

Pauly spun around and did what Ares said—she swam back the way she came, trying to keep as close to him as she could, fighting the current of snow. She held her hand in front of her face so in case she was buried, there would be a pocket around her mouth and nose to breath. At least she'd remembered that from her avalanche training.

The snow had hit her hard. It was cold and moved like heavy, wet cement around her. It went through her snow gear and her legs grew wobbly.

Oh god. Please. I can't leave Jeremy. I can't lose Ares.

She stayed focused on Ares and fought, but her legs gave way.

"No!" Ares shouted and she felt his hands grip her and hold her as they came out of the flow.

She clung to him as they stood back, watching in horror as the snow rushed down the side of the trail, effectively washing the trail away. Finally, it slowed, but they were completely cut off from everyone else and judging by the size of the snow wall in front of them, they were going to be there for a while.

"Pauly, Ares, are you okay?" Greer called over the radio.

"We're good," Ares answered.

"We're calling a snow removal team, but it'll take some time in this weather. There's a cabin, half a kilometer up the trail. It's stocked with wood and you can shelter there."

"We'll do that," Ares replied.

"Keep your radio on."

"Constable, please call the station and have them inform my son we're okay. They know how to find him," Pauly pleaded.

"Copy that," Greer said.

Pauly's body felt like jelly as she tried to catch her breath and process everything that had just happened. Despite how hard it had been, despite the fact that she felt almost like she was going to pass out, being in the field today had felt like she was where she belonged. When she'd gotten into the work, she'd forgotten everything else. It had reminded her of why she loved her job. Though she was worried during that cliff rescue, Ares had it all under control. When the avalanche hit, she'd just focused on Jeremy and Ares and she was here still.

Even though they were trapped that hiker would live. Today, no one was lost in the avalanche and that rush she got from doing the job she loved the most washed through her.

She hated being cut off from Jeremy, but at least she was with Ares. She was safe.

They were alive.

What she tried not to do was focus on Rex and what he might've felt when he was caught in that avalanche. Had he felt the way she had? As soon as she'd thought of it, try as she might, she couldn't get that terror out of her head.

"I've got you," Ares said, reassuringly. He still had his arms wrapped around her.

It eased her mind. Just for a moment as the adrenaline wore off. All she could do was cling to him as she tried to catch her breath.

"Pauly, let's get to the shelter. We need to get warm. Think you can make it?"

"Yeah," she responded and they began the walk up the trail.

The cabin was usually used by backpackers or as an emergency shelter. It had a wood stove and a good supply of firewood, everything to keep warm. It wasn't much, but it was someplace where they could stay out of the storm, which was beginning to worsen, and wait to be dug out.

The main thing was, they were safe.

Albeit cold and tired.

Pauly had never been so terrified in her life as when the snow had come rushing down off the steep rock face. She'd seen avalanches from a distance and she'd been stuck in traffic along a road for hours after one had swept across the highway, but she'd never been in one before today. And all she could think about in that moment was where Ares was and how she didn't want to lose him. How she didn't want to leave Jeremy. So she'd fought with all her might.

Now all she wanted to do was hold on to Ares and have him hold her. She wanted to chase away the terror that her body was letting her feel.

"You stay here and I'll get wood," Ares stated.

She nodded, her teeth chattering. Her boots were full of snow and they had to get some heat going before they succumbed to hyperthermia. Maybe it was just because she was so cold, but she felt like Ares was gone for an eternity. Finally, he came back with an armload of wood. He knelt down in front of the wood stove and piled in the wood. Then he opened his backpack and pulled out a tiny hatchet.

It was an emergency survival kit that he had to carry working with the mountain rescue team. Pauly had never been so glad to see it in her life. He quickly split some of the smaller pieces of wood into kindling and then struck a match and got the fire started.

"I'm going to get another couple loads of wood from the lean-to. I don't think we're going to make it out of here until morning."

Pauly nodded and scooted close to the fire. "You're right."

Ares brought in the wood and then latched the door. The little cabin was basically no bigger than a shed. There was a covered latrine just outside the door, a small bunk and the wood stove. It was meant for roughing it.

Ares dug in his bag and pulled out a couple of vacuum-packed emergency blankets and a sleeping bag.

"You need to get your clothes off," he stated.

"What?" she asked, through chattering teeth.

"Pauly, first rule of hypothermia. Get out of the wet clothes and we'll huddle close for body heat."

"Right." But her heart was racing at the suggestion. It made logical sense, she knew that. The snow had gotten through down to her uniform. Still, the idea of being naked with Ares was making her body thrum with excitement—and a little bit of fear.

He tossed her a blanket then began to peel off his winter clothes as the cabin started to heat up. He had his back to her, but she couldn't help but watch him out of the corner of her eye. She'd seen him with his shirt off, long ago at the beach while they were in college, but this was something different.

She quickly glanced away and tried to get her own clothes off as fast as she could. Once she did that, she wrapped her blanket around herself and scooted to the sleeping bag to sit down on it.

Everything of hers had been wet.

Ares had wrapped his blanket around his waist. His shoulder-length hair was tied back, but she could still see the broad, muscular expanse of his bronzed chest. He picked up the clothes and laid them all out, hanging them up so they could dry by the wood stove.

"That should work. Once they're dry, we can get dressed again and try to get some sleep," he remarked.

"Sounds good," she managed to squeak out, but her mouth had gone dry. All she could do was stare at the way the light from the wood stove played across his chest. There was no other light in the cabin. It wasn't hooked up for electricity, so it was just them, sitting in the darkness, naked and huddled in front of a wood stove.

Ares sat down next to her.

"You need to climb inside this sleeping bag. We need to be close together for…warmth."

Their gazes locked and her breath caught in her throat. She was so close to him, it was intoxicating. All she could think about was being in his arms, the way his lips felt on hers. It had been so long since she felt that intimate connection with someone. Right now, she wanted to be held and comforted.

Why not let it be Ares, her best friend, a man she trusted and loved?

She wanted Ares.

"Are you okay, Pauly?" he asked, his voice trembling slightly.

"I think so."

"What're you thinking about?"

"How much I'd like you to kiss me."

CHAPTER ELEVEN

SHOCK RAN THROUGH ARES, but only for a brief moment, because he wasn't completely certain he'd heard her correctly. And he wanted to make sure it was real.

"You're sure?" he asked.

"Very sure," she said, her voice trembling.

How many times had he wished for this? Longed for this? Too many. It was a dream come true, but he didn't want to take advantage of this situation.

He cleared his throat. "I'd like that too."

Pauly was so close. Her dark hair hung loose, brushing over her soft creamy shoulders and he was well aware that only a blanket separated them. He was so very tempted.

But there was their friendship. He didn't want to hurt her, and he never wanted her to regret this. If they were going to share this moment together, she deserved something special and meaningful. Just like he did. So he hesitated, not wanting to rush her or push her.

Right now, he hated his conscience just a little bit.

"Do you not want to kiss me? You seem hesitant," she questioned.

"It's not that. Not at all. Trust me. I want to kiss you again."

She moved and sat up on her knees, reached out to touch his face. Her soft fingers fired his senses, because her touch was so light, yet it made him want more. It made him burn with need.

"Then what is it?" she asked.

"We're friends."

"Yes."

"It's complicated. I don't want to ruin things, but to tell you the truth… I've always wanted you. I've always been attracted to you." He held back telling her how he also had been in love with her for years. How he'd always dreamed of this moment, even when she belonged to another.

"I want you too, Ares. You're my best friend, I trust you and I want this. I want to share this with you."

He swallowed hard, staring down into her beautiful blue-gray eyes, her body so close to his. He wanted to give her forever in this moment, but he couldn't because he wasn't sure about forever himself. He didn't want to make a promise only to break it later. "I can't promise you anything."

"I understand. I can't promise you anything either, but tonight, I just want to be held again.

And I want you to be the one. I just want… I want you."

"I want you too." And before he could over-think anything, he captured her lips in the kiss that he'd burning to taste once more. The one he couldn't stop thinking about.

For years he'd been fighting his attraction to her, but now, he couldn't hold it back any longer. Pauly wanted him and the need overtook him as he ran his hands over her body, kissing her deeply and fiercely. It was as though all other kisses he'd ever experienced in his life didn't exist.

Only this one.

As much as he wanted to continue, he stopped himself.

"What's wrong?" Pauly asked.

"I don't have protection," he murmured. "Not something I carry around in my emergency kit."

She laughed softly. "I can't get pregnant the usual way."

"What?"

"Blocked fallopian tubes. Rex and I had Jeremy through IVF."

"I didn't know," he replied, softly.

She shrugged. "We didn't share it with many people."

"Are you sure you want to do this?"

She grinned, letting the blanket fall away so he could drink in the sight of her naked body. "Positive."

She pulled him down and he kissed her again, brushing his lips over her soft mouth, over her collarbone, anywhere that he could. He ran his hands across her body, luxuriating in the feel of the silkiness of her skin. It heated his blood to touch her, to be with her here, that she trusted him this much. He wanted her so badly, but he had to pace himself and take his time.

If this was to be his only moment of bliss, a dream come true, he wanted to savor it for as long as possible.

"You make me feel..." he trailed off.

"What?" she asked.

"Alive."

"Same," Pauly said. Her heart was racing. Each kiss, each press of his lips against her skin sent a jolt of pleasure through her. His body was close against hers. They were skin to skin, nothing between them and it felt so right. She'd never really thought she could feel this way again, but she was glad it was with Ares. She trusted him and knew he would never willingly hurt her. He made her feel safe and protected again, which was what she needed more than anything. She opened her legs, arching her hips, wanting him to claim her, take her.

"Pauly, I want you so much," he groaned.

"I'm yours," she panted.

He silenced her words with a deep kiss, their

tongues entwining and she wrapped her legs around his waist. Ares slid his hand between her thighs, stroking her. She cried out as pleasure washed through her. At that moment it felt like the haze that had been controlling her life lifted. She was alive again, she was getting lost in the sensations coursing through her.

"Please," she begged.

"What?" he teased, sliding his tongue around her sensitive nipples.

"I want you."

He groaned and moved his hand. His cock pressed against her entrance and he slowly thrust into her, filling her.

It was overwhelming.

"Damn," he moaned. "You feel so good."

Pauly moved her hips, urging him to move, but he wouldn't. Ares just held her still, buried deep inside her.

"You're a tease," she said.

Ares just chuckled and then he moved, slowly at first, taking his time. Pauly wanted him hard and fast. She wanted to feel all of him. It didn't take long before he quickened his pace, thrusting in and out of her. She met each thrust with her hips, faster and faster and until she could feel her body succumbing to the sweet release she yearned for.

Pleasure overtook her and she cried out his name. Ares's thrusts became shallow until his own release came a moment later.

He rolled off her and she curled up against him, listening to his breathing. It calmed her. This connection was what she'd been craving, for so long.

"Thank you," she whispered, tears stinging her eyes.

"Pauly, are you crying?"

She added. "I'm glad it was you. I needed the comfort after...my life flashed before my eyes out there. Thank you for being here for me."

Ares just wrapped her up in his strong arms. "You're safe. Everything will be okay."

Pauly nodded, closing her eyes and listening to the reassuring beat of his heart. She wanted to believe everything would be okay and stay the same, but she doubted it ever would.

Everything in that moment had changed.

Pauly fell fast asleep in the safety of Ares's arms and slept just as soundly as she did that first night he'd come to live with them. At about seven in the morning, they got a call on the radio that the storm was over and the rescue crew were almost done clearing the path. As much as she didn't want to leave the comfort of this moment with Ares, she had to get dressed and get back to Jeremy. Although he knew they were safe, she was desperate to see him and hold him.

It had been so close a call. Despite her thoughts from the previous night, despite the fact it would kill her to give up field work, she knew it would be better if she stayed behind the desk or the switchboard.

It made her sad, but it was the right thing. The responsible thing. That way she wouldn't have to take any more risks. She'd almost died up there, and the thought of leaving Jeremy alone... Well, it was heartbreaking. She wouldn't let that happen.

She pulled on her warm clothes as Ares roused and got dressed too.

They weren't saying much, but they both had agreed that last night was a onetime thing. They couldn't make any promises to each other. But she couldn't help but wonder what this all meant for their future.

She felt like Ares might be avoiding eye contact, and she hated it. But then their gazes locked and he smiled at her, just like he always did.

Maybe everything would be okay. They might not have forever, but things weren't weird or ruined between them.

Still, she worried about what he would say when she shared her decision about the desk job, because she knew he was against it.

She only hoped he'd still support her and understand her reasons why.

Once they had made sure the fire was out and the cabin was secured, they hiked back down the trail and were met by rescuers and cheers. She'd never been so relieved to see other members of the station house there.

Chief Lloyd was there, smiling. "Of course my best mountain rescuer gets trapped on a simple trail."

Ares chuckled. "Well, it could've been worse."

"We were lucky." Pauly shivered just thinking about that avalanche and the rush of snow that surrounded her. But she only let that thought intrude for a moment. Last night with Ares had helped her chase all that away. Being wrapped up in his warm arms had been so reassuring. It completely grounded her, and reminded her she had survived. She was alive.

"We're going to take you both to the hospital to get you checked out. It's standard protocol, so don't even try to complain," Lloyd stated firmly.

Pauly nodded in agreement, but she really didn't want to go to the emergency room and get checked out. All she wanted to do was get back home and comfort Jeremy. And she wanted to talk to Ares about her decision.

He wasn't going to talk her out of it. That avalanche just firmed her resolve.

Ares sat in a trauma pod in the emergency room. He'd had his evaluation. Now he was just waiting for a doctor's decision, and the all-clear to leave.

He and Pauly had been separated, which was probably for the best at this moment. Things had changed up on that mountain.

It had been amazing having her in his arms all

night. Finally, he'd felt peace. And in the morning, everything was different. When they'd woken up, he'd changed his mind about the promises he said he couldn't make, about how he would never settle down,

Having her, holding her after the avalanche, knowing she was safe when he could've lost her and then making love to her, he'd known for sure what was missing in his life.

Her.

It had always been her. When he watched her almost get swept away by that wall of snow, he'd thought all his dreams were being washed away. It was like everything slowed down and he couldn't move quick enough to save her.

He'd almost lost her and that made him sick to his stomach.

He hadn't been sure what he wanted at first, but now he was certain. If Pauly wanted him, he'd give it all up to be here for her and Jeremy. He was all in.

What if she didn't want it though? It was a terrifying thought.

"Mr. Galanis?" A doctor entered the trauma pod where Ares was waiting.

"Yes."

The doctor looked up from his chart. "Everything is good. I'm discharging you."

"And my partner?" Ares asked.

"Yes. About to do the discharge now."

"Thank you, Doctor." Ares stood up and took the slip of paper from the physician. He walked out of the trauma bay and met Pauly on the way out of the hospital. "All good?"

"Yep," she said. "I'm going to pick Jeremy up now. Do you think you can handle the report?"

"I can do that." His heart was racing and he couldn't get the words out.

"Okay. Well, we'll talk later, right?"

Ares nodded. "Yes. I think we need to."

Pauly left the hospital and Ares scrubbed a hand over his face. He'd done a lot of scary things in his life, but this prospect of declaring his love, changing his life plans, it was probably the most frightening thing of all.

Pauly headed straight for home and then walked to Britt's to pick up Jeremy. It had been hard leaving Ares behind, because she didn't want to let him go, but she knew that she had to. He was safe, as was she.

But in a way it was a relief to have space to figure stuff out. Ares hadn't exactly been chatty since they were rescued, and she was so conflicted about the feelings he was stirring deep inside her.

Right now she didn't want to talk about it. All she wanted to do was be with Jeremy.

"Mom!" Jeremy yelled and came running out to

her, throwing his arms around her. "You okay?"
He was excited, but not crying.

"I am. You're not as upset as you were the other
day?" Pauly wondered, pleasantly surprised.

"Britt told me you were just snowed in a cabin
with Uncle Ari. Where is he?"

"He had to file a report and drop off gear, he
told me to come here and pick you up." She swallowed the lump in her throat. She was glad Jeremy didn't know about the avalanche.

Jeremy nodded. "It was such a big storm. I was
sort of worried."

Pauly smiled and they walked hand in hand
back home. "I'm glad you weren't *too* worried."

"Uncle Ari and I had a talk about it all."

"I didn't know that. Was this that Everest talk?"

Jeremy shrugged. "We talk about a lot of things.
You should talk to him more often. He's cool."

"He definitely is. So tell me about this talk."

"Well, Uncle Ari made me realize how important it is for you to save lives. He told me to be
brave because you and Dad were. Mom, you're
awesome and I want to do what you do when I
grow up. I want to save lives too. Also, I want to
climb Everest."

Pauly's heart swelled. "Wow. I'm so proud of
you, buddy."

"I'm proud of you too, Mom." Jeremy hugged
her tight. "I was scared, but you're okay and it's
okay to be scared."

"I am indeed okay and yes, it's okay to be scared of things."

"Right. It's just how you handle it. Face your fears!" Jeremy said, enthusiastically.

Pauly smiled to herself. Ares had said all that to Jeremy? It meant so much that he talked to him, that he was acting as a strong male role model for him. More than a godfather, but as a friend. As a father.

And, yes, she definitely needed to talk to him, especially about what happened between them last night and what it meant for the future.

He might be stepping up for Jeremy while he was here, but she knew that Ares wasn't ever planning on settling down permanently. If she ever thought about getting into a relationship again, it had to be with someone that was willing to live in Canmore, because she wasn't going to move Jeremy away from where he was happy. From where his last memories of his father were spent. And just as she couldn't risk her heart on someone who wasn't going to stick around, she couldn't put Jeremy at risk of losing another father figure.

Jeremy ran up the stairs and Pauly followed slowly after she took off her coat and kicked off her boots. She had to have a shower and a big cup of coffee. Jeremy had disappeared to his room and she flicked on the coffee maker.

As the coffee percolated, she heard the front door open.

"Ares?" she called out.

"Yeah. It's me." He came up the stairs. "I dropped off the gear and then I picked up some donuts."

"Yum. Want coffee?"

He nodded. "Please."

There was still that awkward tension between them since this morning. Yep, things had definitely gotten weird, but she didn't regret what happened last night. She'd wanted it and she was glad it happened. Now, she could see, it had been building for a while.

"So," Ares said, breaking the silence. "Should we talk?"

She nodded and poured him a cup of coffee. "Yes. I think we better."

"Pauly, I think you know that I care about you deeply…"

"Ares, you don't have to explain anything. I meant what I said, I don't need a promise, so you don't have to make an excuse."

Ares's eyes widened. "I understand that, but…"

"I'm okay." She wrapped her arms around her.

"I know you're okay. Pauly, I'm in love with you."

The words came out so fast and it was unexpected. She almost dropped her mug. "What?"

"I'm in love with you, Pauly. I always have been."

She carefully set her mug down, because she

couldn't quite believe what she was hearing. There was a part of her that was thrilled with his admission, and another that was terrified. She just didn't know how to take it.

"You…love me?"

Ares nodded, his expression pained. "For years. Do you know what it's like to fall in love with your best friend who happens to be married to your other best friend?"

"No," she replied, quietly.

"Pauly, I love you. There's been no other for me."

She worried her bottom lip. She wasn't sure *what* she was feeling. She was so scared of loving again, especially someone she might lose to the mountains like she lost Rex. So scared of being left alone once more. It was too much to handle.

And what terrified her most was that she was falling for him too.

"Ares, I don't know what to say." She could see the disappointment in his face.

Tell him how you feel.

Only, she couldn't get the words out.

"It's okay," he said, quietly. "It's a lot. A lot of things changed, but I wanted you to know how I felt."

"I appreciate that." She tried to muster a brave face. "It's so overwhelming. I've made some decisions of my own too."

He cocked an eyebrow. "Oh?"

Her pulse was thundering in her head. "I'm taking that desk job."

"Why?"

"We could've died up there," she countered.

"But we didn't."

"This time."

"Pauly, every job has risks," he stated.

Pauly shook her head. "I've made up my mind."

"Is it what you want?" he asked.

She paused. No, it really wasn't. She loved being out there in the field, but nothing was going to change her mind. "I won't leave Jeremy alone."

"But he's not. He has us."

"Us?" she asked. "He has me."

"I'm here too."

"For now, but you leave in a year. Or have you decided to actually stay put somewhere?"

Her words stung, but she wasn't completely wrong. There was a time limit to his stay in Canmore. He'd been thinking a lot since they made love and it had taken every ounce of courage he had to tell her how he really felt about her, but she'd responded the way he'd feared she would.

Could he give up his life, his career, for someone who didn't share his feelings? He'd give it all up if she wanted him, but if she didn't feel the same he'd have to move on.

He couldn't stay here and watch her settle down with someone else.

There really wasn't any point in trying. And she wasn't returning the affection. It was clear she wasn't ready to move on. She was scared still. That was okay, but he wasn't sure he could put his life on hold forever on the off chance that one day she'd fall for him too.

Maybe it was just better to stay friends. But right now he wasn't sure their friendship could survive this.

"You're right. I am here temporarily." He got up. "Maybe it's best I go now."

"No," she said, quickly. "Don't do that."

"Why? Because you're afraid to be alone?" Instantly he regretted the words as he said them. Her spine stiffened.

"Why are you running away?" she asked.

"Why are you?"

"I'm not. I'm here. This is my home."

He shook his head. "You're running away from your career, because you're scared about what happened to you as a kid."

"I lost Rex."

"We all did, but at least he died doing what he loved. He didn't let fear rule him."

"You're one to talk," she snapped.

"What do you mean?"

"You're afraid to face your family. You're afraid to live your life because you don't want to be like your father. Why are you so stubborn? Are you so afraid of settling down because of what happened with your parents?"

He opened his mouth to say more, but he heard a shout and saw Jeremy running down the stairs.

"Uncle Ari, I'm glad you're okay!"

Ares plastered a smile on. "Why aren't you in school?"

"Snow day. Want to play a game?" Jeremy asked.

"Sure, pal. I'll be right up there."

Jeremy dashed back upstairs and he turned to look at Pauly. She was looking away, her lips pressed together firmly.

"I'm not the only one scared of change, Pauly." And he left to go upstairs. Their conversation was unfinished, but she was right, he was stubborn and he was scared of making a mistake or driving away the woman he loved. The woman he'd always loved.

And yet, he realized he already done just that. With his confession, he'd driven her away. She wasn't ready and now maybe she'd never be ready.

He'd ruined it all. Just like his father had done to his mother.

CHAPTER TWELVE

ARES COULD SENSE there was some awkwardness between them when they had dinner that night. Thankfully, Jeremy was completely oblivious.

It didn't feel like the blow-out fights that his parents used to have, but he also felt there was a heaviness, a finality in their silence.

There was a part of him that was mad that Pauly was going to take the desk job, that she was too scared to do what she loved, but he also saw her side of it. She was so terrified of leaving Jeremy and he couldn't blame her for that.

And he was thinking about everything else she'd said too. How he was stubborn. He was and he knew it, but what had stung him the most was when she said that he was similar to his father. That was something he had been fighting his whole life, being like his dad or his brothers. Settling down, marrying, and then divorcing.

He'd still turned out exactly like all of them.

Stubborn like a mule, as his *yiayia* would say.

He finished washing up the dishes and Pauly

came back down the stairs, slowly, like she was trying to walk on eggshells. He didn't want her to feel like this in her own home. He didn't want their relationship or friendship to end because of this silly fight. The only thing he could think of that might help was to put some distance between the two of them.

"Is he asleep?" he asked.

"He is. Thanks for doing the dishes."

He shrugged. "I don't mind. You made dinner."

She took a seat at the counter. "Should we finish our conversation?"

He nodded. "I think so. I'm… I'm going to find my own place and then hand in my notice. I could easily hop back into the agency and be sent somewhere else."

Her face was a bit unreadable. "You don't have to do that."

"Well, you won't need me around if you're taking that desk job, and I think some distance would be good."

Pauly frowned. "Look, I know you don't agree with it, but it's the best thing. Rex and I actually talked about it…"

He cocked his head to one side. "Did you really? It just doesn't seem like something Rex would agree to. He knew how much you loved your work, how you liked being out there on the front lines saving lives. Don't deny it."

"I won't be selfish," she snapped. "I have a son I

have to take care of. I won't abandon him, but you wouldn't understand that because you're never going to settle down. You're never going to take on that level of responsibility."

Her words stung, but there was so much truth laid out in those words. He didn't know what it was like. He didn't have a family or kids, because he was terrified of ruining it all.

"No, I guess I'm not," he said, quietly. "Pauly, I don't want to fight."

"I don't want to fight either," she said, her voice breaking. "I don't want to lose you."

"Is it because you love me? Or is it because you don't want to be alone? Really, you can be honest."

"I don't know. Everything has happened so fast…but how can I change everything for someone who can't promise me anything? And I don't expect you to do that, give it all up for me."

It hurt what she said, especially after he'd put himself out there. Ares walked around the counter. He wanted to pull her in his arms and comfort her, but he couldn't.

"I'll see you in the morning, for work."

He had to walk away from her, when all he wanted to do was offer her everything. But she hadn't said that she loved him.

Did she have to? Couldn't he give her time?

When he'd seen her almost be washed away in that avalanche, his life, her life, Jeremy—it had all flashed in front of his eyes. That was what he wanted.

So why couldn't he just let go of this stupid fear of commitment, so that he could have it? Why did she have to reciprocate it right away for him to say he'd stay? What if she needed to hear that first?

Once he was in his room, he saw the letter from his mother.

The letter telling him about his father. The letter that accused him of not answering his phone and it was true, he screened his calls, but his father never called him. Why should he be the one to make amends?

Because you are the bigger person. You're not your father.

That thought smacked him right in his face. And he put himself in his father's shoes. No, he and his father had never really seen eye to eye ever and Ares always felt like a disappointment to him, but he'd never told his father how he felt.

He just walked away because it was easier.

At least, if he reached out now before it was too late, before his father died, he would have that peace of mind knowing that he was the one that had bridged the gap. If his father didn't want to talk, then Ares would know definitively where he stood.

His hands were shaking as he picked up the phone and punched in his father's number. The phone rang.

"Hello?" his father answered on the other end.

"Dad, it's Ares."

There was a moment of silence on the other end. "Aristotle, it's you? Truly?"

Ares rolled his eyes at his father using his full Greek name. Aristotle was such a mouthful; it was why he went by Ares, or Ari to Jeremy. Only his dad would ever use his full name.

"Yes, Dad. It's me. Ares."

"I'm glad you've called me. It's been…a long time."

"It has. I got Mom's letter."

"Ah." His dad sighed on the other end. "I suppose you're going to yell at me about not telling you. Your mother certainly did."

"No. I'm not going to lecture you about it."

"You're not?" his father asked, stunned.

"I'm worried about you," Ares stated, trying to fight the flood of emotion raging through him.

"There's no need to be worried, son. I am glad you called. I wanted to apologize for the way I behaved when you were in college. I was a… I was a fool. It's not easy for me to admit that, but I was foolish. Prideful and stubborn."

Ares laughed softly. "I do understand the stubbornness part. I have been accused of being that too."

His father chuckled. "I think we are more alike than either one of us wants to admit."

"I agree. And I'm sorry for what I said about

the business you built up. I'm sorry I didn't want to take it on, and I'm sorry it's closed."

"It's okay, son. It is in the past. What I'd like is to see you happy. Are you happy with your life, Aristotle—I mean, Ares?"

The question caught Ares off guard. Everything that had happened since college played through his mind. There were moments where he had felt happy and proud, but they were few and far between. His life was lonely. He'd tried to fill that void, that hole in his heart with other things, but... No, he wasn't particularly happy.

There was more that he wanted. Most of all, he wanted to be with Pauly and Jeremy. He'd always miss Rex, but he wanted to take care of them. He wanted a family with them, here in Alberta. He just had to fight to get it.

"I think I will be," he said.

"Good. That is all I ever wanted for my children and my grandchildren."

"I'll fly out and visit you as soon as I get some time off. Things are a bit busy with all the snow and avalanches."

"Avalanches? Are you being careful?" his father asked.

"I am. I'm part of a mountain rescue team."

"Well, they certainly should have you on that team. You scaled Everest."

"How...how did you know that?" Ares asked, stunned.

"Your mother showed me a picture."

Emotion flooded through him and he fought back tears. "You and Mom talk?"

"A lot has changed in the last decade or so," his father said, gently. "We still care for each other—we just don't want to be married anymore. Though, the amount she comes around and pesters me it's like she is still married to me. She's my best friend."

Ares swallowed the hard lump in his throat. "I have to go. But I'll call you again, Dad. I love you."

"I love you too, son." His father's voice broke. "Thank you for calling me. We'll talk again soon."

Ares ended the call and ran his hand over his face. He had a sense of loss, of grief for the years they'd both managed to waste. But with what time his father had left he was going to make sure it counted. And he was going to fight for a life with Pauly.

This time he wasn't going to run away.

Pauly was his best friend and he wasn't going to let that go. Even if she didn't want to have a romantic relationship with him right now, he was still going to be here for her. He wasn't going to let his pride stand in the way.

He wasn't going to abandon her.

He couldn't, because he loved her and that's what counted. If he had to wait for her, he would. He just wanted her in his life.

* * *

Why didn't I tell him I loved him back?

Pauly was wrestling with that little voice in her head. Right now it was berating her for not telling Ares how she felt. Instead, she'd just come up with excuses. But when he said he was going to leave, it had scared her. She didn't want him to go.

But it was hard to even contemplate moving on with someone else, someone she cared for deeply.

When Rex had died it had crushed her to her very core.

And, since then, she'd just existed, numb.

When it came to Jeremy, she put on a brave face for him, because she had to. She wanted his life to be as normal as possible, but in the process of trying to keep things that way, she'd been burying her own emotions.

Grief. Anger. Loneliness.

And then Ares had come into her and Jeremy's life and there was happiness and laugher again. She didn't know what it was that sent Ares to her when she needed him the most, but she was thankful.

The problem was now she was worried that she'd ruined it all. That she'd driven him away, because she was so scared of telling him how she felt. Telling him that she loved him too. That she was terrified to act on it, because what if she lost him?

What if she lost her best friend?

I'd be alone again.

It didn't have to do with the guilt of moving on. She and Rex had even talked about that once. They'd both agreed that, if either of them died young, they'd be happier knowing the one left behind might find love again. It was about making space in your heart to allow that to happen.

She would always love Rex. He was her first love, her first everything. But now she was in love with Ares too.

She just wasn't sure if he would stick around long-term.

"What do I do?" she wondered out loud, staring at her bedroom window. She could see a ski hill all lit up and little black dots whizzing down the hill in the distance. People. It always gave her some comfort to watch them.

It was the mountain where she spread Rex's ashes. The mountain where he lost his life doing what he loved.

Is Ares right? Can I really give up the job I love?

"Rex, what do I do?" she asked again, dropping her head into her hand. In this moment, she felt like that lost little girl again. She and her parents might have worked that all out years ago, but there were still times when she felt so alone.

"Mom?"

Pauly spun around, wiping the tears from her

eyes to see Jeremy standing in the doorway. "What're you doing awake?"

"You were talking to Daddy." Jeremy came into the room and climbed up on her bed so he could see out the window. "I talk to him too."

She smiled and took a seat next to him. "I'm glad that you do."

"I also like talking to Ari," Jeremy stated. "He loves us. Both of us."

"I know he does," she replied softly.

"I want him to stay. Forever."

"You do?"

Jeremy nodded. "At Daddy's funeral, he talked to me. He told me that Daddy was one of his best friends, you were his other best friend and that I could be his best friend too. Best friends should stick together."

She wiped away another tear. "You're right. They should."

"You love him too. Don't you?" Jeremy asked. "Uncle Ari, I mean."

Her heart began to race. "I think I do. Would it make you angry if Ares did stick around forever and lived with us? If we maybe become a family?"

"No!" Jeremy said, smiling. "I think that's what Daddy would want."

"And you'd like that?"

"Mommy, you're sad. Uncle Ari makes you happy. We're family and don't families stay together?"

Pauly pulled him into a hug. "They do. But you know we do the same kind of job, right? Are you really okay with that? Are you okay with Mommy *and* Uncle Ari out there together?"

"Yep. He told me. You, him and Daddy all save lives. That's cool. You have to help people who are injured or stuck. You can't give that up. If you do, then who will help those people who need you?"

"Good point." Pauly kissed the top of his head. "You're smart."

"I know," Jeremy stated.

Just then there was a rumble. It shook the whole house. Holding Jeremy close, Pauly turned to see the mountain, where the little skiers had been moments ago, had been eclipsed by a torrent of white, rushing down the hill like a tsunami.

Her stomach sank and her heart began to race. She couldn't believe what she was seeing and for a moment she felt the bite of the cold snow against her skin, the force of it trying to drag her down.

You're okay.

"Mommy!" Jeremy whispered.

"I know, buddy. I know." Her world was spinning out of control.

Ares came rushing upstairs and into the room, obviously hearing the roar. "What… Oh my god."

He came to stare out the window at the snow tumbling down.

Pauly pursed her lips together and they watched as the snow covered the ski lodge and all those skiers. It finally ended and as soon as it did her work phone rang, as did Ares's. Ares stepped out in the hall to answer.

Pauly picked hers up, her hands shaking. "Pauly speaking."

"It's Lloyd. We're calling everyone in."

"I figured so. I'll be there as soon as I get Jeremy off to the sitter."

"Thanks, Pauly."

Pauly ended the call and turned to Jeremy. "I have to go. I'm going to take you to Britt."

Jeremy nodded. "I'll go pack and change. You go help those people, Mommy."

He ran off and Pauly texted Britt. Britt would understand—her husband was Fire. He'd be called in too, along with all emergency service people in the area. Everyone would be needed on that mountain.

Ares came back in the room and for a minute her pulse began to race, thinking of the decision she'd just made. Everything she wanted with him.

Then she saw his face and worry blotted all of that out. "So, I guess we're both back on duty."

He'd be doing some of the riskier rescues. The thought filled her with dread, especially now that she knew how she felt. She might lose him today, right when she'd decided she couldn't live without him.

If she dwelled on the fear, she wouldn't be able to save lives.

"Yep. It's all hands on deck."

"Okay. Get changed and we'll go after we drop off Jeremy."

Ares nodded and then left.

Pauly took a deep breath and looked at the mountain. It was going to be hard working up there, but she had to put all her fear, all her anxiety aside and do her job.

And she knew one thing for certain—this wouldn't be the last time.

She'd tell Ares about it all later, but she wasn't walking away from the job she loved because of fear. And she wasn't walking away from him either.

When the time was right, she'd tell him how she felt and how she wasn't going to let him go. She wanted a second chance at life and she wanted it with him.

They were risking their lives tonight, but it was worth it. She just hoped that at the end of this tragedy, there'd be happiness for them all.

CHAPTER THIRTEEN

PAULY GOT JEREMY to Britt's house then she and Ares traveled to the station house. So much for their day off to recuperate from their own avalanche experience. But when it was an emergency situation like this, everyone was needed. Every hand counted. And although Pauly was wrestling with her feelings, her new realization, now was not the time and place to discuss it. They had to stay focused and stay collected to do their jobs.

The moment they got to the station house the chief, Lloyd was there.

"Pack all your emergency gear. Teams from Banff, Kannaskis and Calgary are en route. The Canadian Armed Forces have been called in. There is a triage center being erected on site. You will be picking up teams of trauma doctors from the Canmore hospital to take up to the site and they will direct you on which patients to bring back down the mountain. We're preparing for the worst. One ski lodge was buried. Those with mountain experience, you will be headed out onto the snow pack to listen for avalanche beacons. Stick together and stay safe."

Pauly and Ares didn't say much to each other as they loaded the back of the ambulance with the equipment he would need to traverse up the snowpack. Just the thought of him being up there made Pauly's fingers tremble, but he was one of the qualified candidates to do that job. The uncertainty of it all filled her with dread, but much like he'd told Jeremy, she had to be brave so he could do his work and save as many lives as possible.

Still, it was hard not to think about the dangers. Even after an avalanche settled, if the angle of the slope was right, it could give way again, or the snow pack could be deceptive and rescuers could be buried themselves.

But there were lives that needed saving out on that hill. This was why they became paramedics.

"You ready?" Ares asked, breaking the silence.

"As ready as I'll ever be." She offered him a brave smile. "Let's get this done."

He nodded.

They climbed into their rig and headed straight for the hospital. The first team of doctors were ready with their gear and dressed for outside. Once they'd piled into the rig, they made their way to the barricaded road outside of town.

Fire and the RCMP had blocked the road leading to the mountain.

As they approached the barricade and were let

through, navigating drifts of snow, Pauly held her breath, her pulse hammering between her ears. It was like nothing she'd ever seen in Canmore.

This road led to one of the more elite ski lodges in the Canmore area, and it was usually plowed and lined by beautiful trees. In the summer, when they offered up tree-top trekking and obstacle course types of events, the roadside would be bursting with flowers.

Now trees were knocked over, snapped like twigs, their branches stripped bare by the first of the snow.

Other emergency crews were plowing out the snow that had partially covered the road.

"This is awful," Pauly murmured, gripping the wheel tighter.

"This will be bad," Ares said.

"Have you ever worked a natural disaster before?" she asked.

"Yep. Hurricanes." He sighed. "Have you?"

"Forest fires, but nothing quite like this." She craned her head to look at a dangerously low-hanging power line, but the top of the rig wasn't going to catch it.

When they reached what used to be the main parking lot of the ski lodge, they were stopped by a member of the military.

"You have doctors?" The corporal asked when Pauly rolled down her window.

"Yep."

"We're having all ambulances park over there by the tent we set up. We have crews excavating the buried ski lodge and bringing out the wounded. Back in so that you're able to leave quickly and we'll make sure you're not boxed in," the corporal stated, gesturing to where the makeshift hospital was set.

"Thank you," Pauly replied.

She drove over to where she was told to park and backed in. After she parked, they opened up the rear doors and let the medical team out. Ares grabbed his gear from the back.

All Pauly could do was watch. Her stomach was in knots and she wanted to stop him, to keep him safe.

There was so much she wanted to do or say, but this wasn't the time or the place.

The corporal who had directed them came over to them now. "I was told one of you is experienced with mountain climbing?"

"I am part of that team," Ares said. "I'm ready, just tell me where to go."

"I'll take you there right now," the corporal said. "We're only having experienced climbers traverse the snow pack."

Ares nodded. "Lead the way, Corporal."

As he turned to walk away, Pauly grabbed his arm, not wanting to let go. She wanted to keep him safe. Ares paused and looked down at her.

"Be careful," she said, hoping her voice didn't

break. And then she completely broke work protocol and kissed him, telling him how she felt in that kiss. All the words she wanted to say, but couldn't. "Be safe."

Ares touched her face gently, his expression soft. Something had changed and she hoped he knew how she felt in that moment. Maybe, just maybe he felt what she was feeling. "I will come back to you. I promise."

"You will."

He smiled, his eyes twinkling with warmth. "Yes. Always."

Pauly nodded and watched him disappear.

It was breaking her heart that he was leaving her, but she knew that he would come back. She had to keep focused on that. She couldn't have it any other way. She couldn't lose him. She couldn't save Rex, but he'd died doing what he loved. He never gave up and Pauly couldn't control everything. Uncertainty was a part of life.

She couldn't even control her feelings for Ares. But she could control how she acted.

She loved him and when he came back down, after all this was over, she was going to tell him how she felt. That even if he wanted to continue his work traveling the world, she didn't care. They could still be together. That was all she cared about in this moment.

That they were together.

Forever.

* * *

The imprint of Pauly's lips were still burned on his, her taste still lingering on his tongue. Although she didn't say it, everything was in that kiss and he knew how she felt. When he made her that promise that he'd come back to her, he meant it.

Right now, he had to push those thoughts aside to work with the rescue team. When they got to the main site Ares was in awe, but also horrified at the size of the snow pack. What was left of the ski hill, everything that wasn't buried under the snow, was a mess. The ski lift was a tangled heap and the big lights that lit up the hill were on their sides.

There were electrical crews out there, trying to make sure the downed wires were safe.

"Do we know how many are unaccounted for?" Ares asked, as they were gearing up to head out there and search for beacons.

"Fifteen are missing out of the list of those who were on the hill tonight," the head of mountain rescue stated. "The resort requires all skiers to carry an avalanche beacon. You have your probes. Once you locate a beacon with the transceiver, use the probe to search for the victim. When they have been located leave the probe in the snow and shovel downward."

Ares headed out carefully on the pack.

Only fifteen people unaccounted for. The mountain rescue team was at least twenty-five strong. They had to work quickly.

As Ares started his search all he could think about was Rex. He'd been doing a rescue just like this when a second avalanche had hit and even though he'd pulled his beacon, he had hit his head on a rock and died. It hurt to know that Rex had done everything right, but a twist of fate, a rock in the wrong spot, had ended his life.

But as Ares worked, he also thought of Rex by his side. Rex lived, loved and worked in these mountains and he'd wanted Ares to be there too. Although this wasn't the mountain where Rex had died, Ares felt his spirit was tied to the Rockies.

He'd always felt like that, even before Rex died. Even though Ares wandered, Rex and the Rockies had always been a beacon, calling him back. And Pauly had always been a safe harbor.

Now it was like Rex was here beside him, guiding him as he worked, just like always. Like he'd been by Ares's side when they had been climbing.

"Do you think we'll ever tire of this, Rex?" Ares asked as they sat on a cliff after finally getting to the top of the summit. They had just finished their climb of Mount Edith Cavill together.

"Nah," Rex responded, smiling. "I hope to bring Jeremy out here one day. Pauly too. I'll never get sick of it." He glanced at Ares. "I'm going to die on these mountains."

"Why would you say that?"

Rex shrugged. "It's something I've known for a long time. I want to to die on the mountain. I belong here. I don't want to die in a hospital bed or my sleep. I want to die doing what I love."

"I don't think Pauly would appreciate that much," Ares teased.

Rex laughed softly. "Well, I don't plan on it happening anytime soon. But, when it does, my ashes need to be spread on a mountain, okay?"

"Okay, fair enough."

"Don't get me wrong, I'm not ready to go yet. I love my life, my family, and I love mountain rescue. I'm telling you, you need to come here and do this with me. We could be unstoppable, eh?" Rex grinned. "Saving lives. Together."

"I love my freedom to travel too much."

"I get that." Rex sighed. "Still, when I'm out here I think about all three of us. You, me, Pauly doing what we love on the mountain. That would be a dream."

Now Rex was gone and even though he'd gone out the way that he wanted, there were times that Ares regretted not coming here sooner and working with him. But as he worked here now, he could feel his late friend.

He could feel the very essence of him in this place, the place he loved most of all.

And it was almost like he could hear his voice saying, *"I'm right here, buddy. Always by your side. I got your back."*

Now, Ares would have his, and take care of Rex's family.

Ares moved his probe over the snow. It wasn't long before he got a hit on his transceiver. Using his probe, he searched in the standard radius pattern from the lowest point, probing the snow until he found who he was looking for. Ares signaled to his partner that he had a positive hit for a beacon. He pulled out his shovel and began digging, under the probe, working carefully so he didn't injure whoever was buried under the pack.

There was a little pocket of air and the person rolled out, unconscious, but breathing.

Ares knelt down in the snow and checked for vitals. "You're okay. We'll get you down."

The woman groaned.

"I need a stretcher," Ares called out, and his partner waved to signal to members of the team who weren't sweeping the pack that they had someone who needed to be taken to triage.

Ares helped load the woman up and they got her off the snow pack and down to the triage area. As he removed his probe from the snow pack, he looked around and saw more people being pulled out. Some hadn't been completely buried in a depression.

One down. Fourteen to go.

Pauly worked with the doctors in the triage area. While the doctors focused on the more seriously injured, Pauly was able to triage and treat those that were being brought down from the buried ski lodge and from the snow pack. Thankfully, a lot of them had minor injuries and those with serious injuries were being sent to the hospital, by air lift.

The Armed Forces had brought one of their helicopters and there was a clear pad to airlift the really injured victims to Calgary, because most of Canmore's medical team was up on the mountain currently.

Pauly was able to wrap up minor cuts and bruises and there were enough paramedics on the scene to shuttle doctors back to the hospital and some of the patients back down the mountain. One of the head doctors in the makeshift triage area wanted Pauly there to direct patients and she was only too glad to stay and assist.

She had no problem driving a patient to the hospital if it was needed, but really she wanted to stay up on the mountain until she was sure that Ares had gotten down okay. She could see the rescuers out on the snow pack, from a distance; she was impressed by how efficiently they were working and the fact that they were finding so many people.

The first woman to be brought into triage only had a minor concussion and they got her off in an ambulance straight away. However, some of the people they were pulling from the ski lodge weren't so lucky.

While her body moved quickly and efficiently, handling patients, all she could think of was Ares. When he came down, she was going to do more than kiss him. She was going to make up for her hesitation and tell him she loved him and wanted a life with him. No more wasting time.

She heard crying and turned to see a little girl, standing by herself, wrapped in a blanket.

"Are you okay?" she asked, kneeling in front of the little girl.

"I was screaming outside. Mommy said don't yell, I could cause an avalanche and then…and now… My mommy is missing!"

Pauly wrapped the blanket around the little girl tighter. "I've got you. My name is Pauly and I'm a paramedic. Can I check to see if you have any cuts or scrapes?"

The little girl nodded.

Pauly picked her up and carried her to her rig, where it was warm and bright and she had a gurney. She set the little girl down.

"What's your name?" Pauly asked.

"Mary."

"Mary is a nice name. Does anywhere hurt?"

"My leg," Mary responded.

"Can I look?"

Mary nodded. Pauly examined her leg and saw some bruising and a deep cut that would need stitching. "Ouch, we're going to get some antibiotics on it and bandage it, then we're going to get you to the hospital."

"I can't leave without my mommy," Mary sobbed.

"What's your mommy's name?"

"Heather," Mary responded.

"Okay, we're going to bandage you up, then see if we can find her and then we'll get both of you to the hospital."

"Okay," Mary responded. "I don't want to be alone. I'm scared."

Pauly felt her heart break, just for a moment, because right then she was transported back to when she was a child. When she had been the one standing, all alone, crying. And all the times she felt that loneliness over the years.

Every time she felt that, she was that same lost little girl, like Mary.

But not anymore.

Ever since Ares had come into her life, she hadn't been alone. She no longer had to shoulder all the burden and take care of everything. He'd been so good to Jeremy, talking to him, supporting him and her. They were partners in every sense of the word.

In that moment, she realized she could make anything work as long as Ares was in her life. She could see it all now with crystal clarity.

"You're not alone," she told Mary, and for once

she believed it for herself too. "I'm here and there are so many people out there helping."

Mary nodded. "Did I do this?"

"No," Pauly responded quickly. "Avalanches happen because of snow. Too much snow. It's been snowing a lot. Are you from Canmore?"

"No. I'm from Victoria."

"British Columbia?" Pauly asked, trying to distract the girl.

"Yep."

"So you have mountains, maybe not the snowfall like we get. Well, you have to have a lot of snow and then the temperatures have to be just right. It gets to a point that the mountain just can't hold all that snow any longer and it breaks away."

"Oh."

"So you see, your little scream didn't cause this."

Mary smiled tearfully. "Oh good. I'm glad."

"Mary?" a woman called out, frantically. "Mary? Answer me!"

"That's my mom. Mom!" Mary shouted.

Mary's mother spun around and came rushing to the ambulance, the relief palpable on her face. "Oh my god, Mary. You're okay?"

Mary wrapped her chubby arms around her mom. "I'm okay, Mom."

"She has a deep laceration," Pauly responded. "I stopped the bleeding, but she's going to need stitches and possibly a tetanus booster or antibiotics. I cleaned it and bandaged it, but she might need to be checked out for a break. She's not walking very well. I would like to take you both to the hospital."

Heather nodded. "It's just us two on vacation here. I was terrified when that…"

"I didn't cause it, Mom," Mary said proudly.

Heather kissed Mary on the top of her head. "I'm sorry I yelled at you."

"Can we go now?" Mary asked, Pauly. "Mommy is here and I don't feel so good."

"Sure thing," Pauly said. She got Heather and Mary secured and then let the corporal in charge of the triage area know she was transporting a patient and her daughter to the Canmore hospital.

Once everything was ready to go she left the accident site and did the patient transfer down to the Canmore hospital by herself. Alone, but not lonely. And though it bothered her to leave Ares up there on the mountain, she knew he could handle himself. He'd promised he'd come back and she believed him.

"This is our last shift together," Ares stated.

"What?" Pauly asked, distracted.

"We graduate in a couple of weeks."

"Right." She worried her bottom lip. "It's going to be weird."

"What is?" Ares asked, finishing up some paperwork.

"Us. All going our separate ways." She glanced

down at the engagement ring on her hand, think-
ing about the life she and Rex were going to lead.
"It'll be weird not having you as my partner."

Ares smiled and he nodded. "We make a good
team."

"We do. And it'll be weird we won't all be liv-
ing together anymore."

A strange expression flashed across his face.
"I know, but you and Rex are getting married.
You don't need me as a third wheel."

"Ares, you're one of my best friends."

Ares stood up and pulled her into a hug. "I'll
always be that, Pauly. I won't abandon you or
Rex."

"Promise?" she asked, holding tight to her
partner, to her friend. Wondering where this next
chapter would take him.

"Always."

Just thinking back to that caused Pauly's eyes
to fill with tears. He'd always been there for her,
just like he promised. She couldn't let him walk
out of her life. So when he came down off that
mountain she was going to make everything right.

She was tired of being too scared, of worrying
about everything that she couldn't control. All
she could do was take life one day at a time and
she wanted Ares by her side when she did that.

It was a long wait at the hospital, but she got Mary
and Heather transferred and then she went back

up to the mountain. She did a few more transfers, then, when it was almost midnight and she was on yet another trip back up to the hill, she learned that the last of the missing people had been found and retrieved. All the rescuers were coming down off the mountain.

Everyone had been extracted from the ski lodge, as well. Soon they would be able to start transporting the doctors and the remaining patients back down the hill.

It would take days for the cleanup to happen, but as far as Pauly heard, no one had died, which was kind of a miracle.

She waited, somewhat impatiently, for Ares to return. She wanted to set everything right. Even though there was no guarantee it would work out forever, she knew there would be no hope unless she took the chance. It was risky, but she was ready.

When she finally saw him walk through the tent, she was ecstatic. Her heart began to race in anticipation. Their eyes locked across the tent and it took everything in her not to run up to him and throw her arms around him, but they had doctors to transport back to town.

This wasn't the time and place.

"Hi," he said, his eyes shining and his smile so warm.

"You came back." Her voice broke.

"Just like I promised."

She nodded. "We have to take the team of doctors back to the hospital and then go to the station house."

"Let's go then."

Her pulse was racing and relief washed through her. Somehow she knew it would all be okay.

They didn't say too much more to each other. They got the doctors settled and then Pauly drove the rig back into town. Once the doctors had been dropped off at the hospital, they headed straight for the station where they off-loaded their gear and made their reports.

Separately.

It was two in the morning by the time they were done and able to head back home.

"You going to pick up Jeremy?" Ares asked.

"No, I think I'll let him sleep. I let Britt know, and that her husband, Ernie, is okay and still up there."

"It's going to take a long time to clean up."

She nodded and parked the truck. "It will indeed."

They headed back into her house and Ares went to go in his bedroom, but Pauly grabbed his arm.

"I think we need to talk," she said, hoping her voice didn't tremble. "There's a lot to say."

"Sure. I want to talk too, but I thought you might be tired."

"I think I have a bit too much adrenaline after the last couple of days."

They headed up into the kitchen and Pauly put the kettle on and set out two mugs. It was out of habit, because her heart was racing thinking about what she wanted to talk to him about.

"So, you kissed me," Ares started. "I wasn't expecting that, but...it meant a lot."

"I did, because I wanted to tell you I love you, and it was hard around everyone and with the work we had to do. I just couldn't let you go without letting you know, some way, how I feel."

Ares eyes widened. "You...you love me?"

She nodded again. The kettle whistled and she quickly shut it off, turning her back to him and taking a deep breath. As she stood there, Ares came up behind her and placed his hand on the small of her back; she turned back around to face him.

"You know how I feel."

"I do." She swallowed. "And I know how much you love your life, your freedom. I know that you always swore off getting married since your parents divorced."

"I know I did, but here's the thing, Pauly. I've been in love with you for a long time, but you loved Rex and I cared for both of you. I never wanted to come between you and...it was hard for me to tell you how I felt, especially with Rex gone."

"I understand. It was hard for me to admit it too. I've always cared for you. I've always been close to you and it was hard for me to even think about opening my heart again, but there's room for you both and I can't think of a better man, than you. I do love you and I'm willing to give this a try, even if you continue your work and travel."

"But, you don't like to be alone."

"I'm not alone though," she said, quickly. "Not if I have you."

Ares couldn't believe what she was saying. He was thrilled, because this was everything he'd hoped for. Pauly was in love with him, she didn't care if he wanted to keep wandering, they could be together.

The only thing was, he didn't *want* to continue to live his transient life.

Not anymore.

"I don't expect marriage or for you to settle down with me. I know it's a lot with Jeremy and…"

Ares silenced her speaking with a tender kiss. "I want that."

"What?" she whispered.

"I want a life with you and Jeremy. I want to be settled down. I loved what I did, but I want to plant roots. And, when you're ready, I want to be married to you. I want to take care of you and Jeremy."

"You do?" she asked, softly.

"Yes."

"What happened to change your mind?"

"I called my father," he said.

"You did? How did that go?"

Ares smiled. "Good. I apologized to him and he apologized to me and I think… I think things are going to work out. I took my anger out on him by swearing off everything he thought a good life stood for—the career he wanted for me, settling down. I was scared, too, about marriage because my parents did love each other at one time and seeing that turn to hate and animosity…it was too much to bear. Then my brothers both had failed marriages, and my sister's started disintegrating too. I didn't want that. And I didn't want that for us, but I can't live without you, Pauly."

A tear slid down her face and he brushed it away with the pad of his thumb.

"I want to marry you, Pauly. And I want to stay here in Canmore with you and Jeremy. If you'll have me."

She nodded, smiling. "I would like that too. I never thought that I would fall in love again. I wasn't expecting to, but you made me see there is more to life than grief, worry and sadness. I love you so very much, Ares."

Cupping her face, he bent down and captured her lips in a kiss. He was still shaking, because he didn't know what the future was going to hold, but he was glad that he was going to be able to do it with Pauly.

The woman he'd always loved.

"Jeremy is going to be thrilled," she murmured, leaning her head against his chest as he held her, stroking his back.

"I hope so."

"Of course he will. He adores you."

"He can still call me Uncle Ari if he wants too. I don't expect anything else. I wonder if I'm still a godparent if I'm a stepparent?"

"I think both," Pauly laughed. "How about we go to bed?"

Ares cocked an eyebrow. "Your place or mine?"

Pauly kissed him again. "How about ours?"

EPILOGUE

Summer, Calgary

ARES WAS ANXIOUSLY waiting at the airport. At least it wasn't as cold as the first day that he arrived. Pauly and Jeremy were with him, for moral support, but he was still nervous about this incoming flight.

Although Pauly had met his mother, she hadn't met his father. Only Rex had met both of his parents. They'd really liked Rex and had mourned his loss, just as Ares had. So they couldn't wait to meet Jeremy.

And now both of them were coming in from Toronto.

Together.

And, honestly, he felt bad for the flight attendants.

"They'll be fine," Pauly said, reassuringly rubbing his arm.

"I know they'll be fine. It's everyone else on

the plane. I was surprised that they both wanted to travel to our wedding together."

"I think it's nice."

Ares widened his eyes. "Be prepared for some loudness in your house for the next couple of days."

"I'm definitely prepared for that," Pauly teased. "Between you and Jeremy, I think I can handle my new in-laws."

"You might change your mind about marrying me." He was half teasing.

"Doubtful."

Jeremy came running over. "What do I call your parents, Ari?"

"I don't know, pal. Knowing my mom she might want to be called *yiayia*," Ares replied.

"*Yiayia*," Jeremy repeated slowly. "That means grandma, right?"

Ares nodded. "You got it, pal."

"Cool."

The arrival doors opened and instantly Ares could hear his parents through the din of other people coming off the plane. Pauly was silently laughing behind her hand as Ares walked forward to find his parents waving their arms around and talking very loudly and quickly.

As soon as his mother saw him, she called out his name and wrapped her arms around him, kissing him.

"You're finally getting married. Where's Pauly?

I told you she was a good girl!" His mother moved on and saw Pauly and went to hug her and kiss her.

Ares went to his father. He looked a little more frail, but overall he wasn't in too bad of shape for someone who was battling cancer. Ares was just thankful that he was here and able to celebrate his wedding to Pauly.

"You're looking good, son." His father hugged him. "I'm glad you're getting married to the right woman."

"I am too. I'm glad you're here."

"So am I. Now, apparently I have a new grandson?" his father asked.

Ares turned and saw that Jeremy was being accosted by his mother. She had a hold of his cheeks and was kissing him and rubbing Jeremy's red head. "Uh, that's Jeremy."

His father chuckled. "It looks like Yiayia got a hold of him. He does look like Rex."

"He does, but he's got a lot of his mother in him too."

"So do you. So like your mother." His father clapped him on his back and went over to meet Jeremy. Ares heard his father say, "I'm your *papou*!"

Then his father turned to Pauly and gave her a hug and a kiss on the cheek.

As his parents fussed over Jeremy, Pauly and Ares grabbed their luggage and then they all walked out of the airport toward the parking garage.

"Yiayia and Papou. Grandma and Grandpa, right?" Pauly asked.

Ares nodded. "Yep."

"Good. I'm going to have to get used to that, especially when our baby starts talking." She walked ahead and Ares froze, not sure if he heard her correctly, but hoping he did.

"Our what?" he asked.

Pauly turned around and smiled at him. "Our baby. I found out this morning. My doctor called."

"I thought...blocked fallopian tubes."

She nodded. "I know. I guess one got through. I made sure that it wasn't ectopic. I wanted to be certain that everything was okay before I told you, but everything is good and in eight months or so we're going to have a baby. Now I'll really have to take a desk job, but only for a short time. I'm not giving up completely."

"I never expected you would."

"So," she asked, her voice filled with a bit of trepidation. "How do you feel about it?"

Ares let go of the luggage and picked her up in his arms, kissing her and laughing. "Are you serious?"

"Very serious."

Ares kissed her again, slowly, just overcome with complete joy. "I love it. I love you and our new baby. I can't wait."

"What's going on you two?" his mother asked. "Can't you wait until the wedding?"

"Shall we tell them?" Pauly asked.

Ares nodded and set her down, putting his arm around her. "Pauly just told me, she's pregnant. So I guess we couldn't wait for the wedding."

"I'm going to be a big brother?" Jeremy asked. "Awesome." He ran up to hug them.

"A baby?" his mother shrieked. "I'm so happy!"

His father was grinning and then said. "Maria, let's celebrate at a restaurant. I'm starving."

"Yes, let's go have something to eat," Ares agreed.

"Let's go to the bowling alley! They have great pizza," Jeremy stated.

"Maybe some other time," Ares said, laughing. "Take your *yiayia*'s suitcase."

Jeremy nodded and took over the suitcase, rolling it, following behind his new grandparents. Ares slung his arm around Pauly.

"You happy?" she asked.

"Yes. I have everything I've ever wanted."

She cocked an eyebrow. "That's not what you said in college."

"Well, I was a fool then."

"And now?" she teased.

"I'm just a fool for you."

* * * * *

*If you enjoyed this story, check out these
other great reads from Amy Ruttan*

Their Accidental Vegas Vows
Rebel Doctor's Boston Reunion
Tempted by the Single Dad Next Door
Reunited with Her Off-Limits Surgeon

All available now!

Get up to 4 Free Books!

**We'll send you 2 free books from each series you try
PLUS a free Mystery Gift.**

FORGOTTEN GREEK PROPOSAL

HIS ROYAL BRIDE REPLACEMENT

FREE Value Over **$25**

Finding a Family Next Door

A Kiss Under the Northern Lights

Both the **Harlequin Presents** and **Harlequin Medical Romance** series feature exciting stories of passion and drama.

YES! Please send me 2 FREE novels from Harlequin Presents or Harlequin Medical Romance and my FREE gift (gift is worth about $10 retail). After receiving them, if I don't wish to receive any more books, I can return the shipping statement marked "cancel." If I don't cancel, I will receive 6 brand-new larger-print novels every month and be billed just $7.19 each in the U.S., or $7.99 each in Canada, or 4 brand-new Harlequin Medical Romance Larger-Print books every month and be billed just $7.19 each in the U.S. or $7.99 each in Canada, a savings of 20% off the cover price. It's quite a bargain! Shipping and handling is just 50¢ per book in the U.S. and $1.25 per book in Canada.* I understand that accepting the 2 free books and gift places me under no obligation to buy anything. I can always return a shipment and cancel at any time. The free books and gift are mine to keep no matter what I decide.

Choose one: ☐ **Harlequin Presents Larger-Print** (176/376 BPA G36Y)   ☐ **Harlequin Medical Romance** (171/371 BPA G36Y)   ☐ **Or Try Both!** (176/376 & 171/371 BPA G36Z)

Name (please print)

Address   Apt. #

City   State/Province   Zip/Postal Code

Email: Please check this box ☐ if you would like to receive newsletters and promotional emails from Harlequin Enterprises ULC and its affiliates. You can unsubscribe anytime.

| Mail to the **Harlequin Reader Service:** |
| **IN U.S.A.:** P.O. Box 1341, Buffalo, NY 14240-8531 |
| **IN CANADA:** P.O. Box 603, Fort Erie, Ontario L2A 5X3 |

Want to explore our other series or interested in ebooks? Visit www.ReaderService.com or call 1-800-873-8635.

---

*Terms and prices subject to change without notice. Prices do not include sales taxes, which will be charged (if applicable) based on your state or country of residence. Canadian residents will be charged applicable taxes. Offer not valid in Quebec. This offer is limited to one order per household. Books received may not be as shown. Not valid for current subscribers to the Harlequin Presents or Harlequin Medical Romance series. All orders subject to approval. Credit or debit balances in a customer's account(s) may be offset by any other outstanding balance owed by or to the customer. Please allow 4 to 6 weeks for delivery. Offer available while quantities last.

Your Privacy—Your information is being collected by Harlequin Enterprises ULC, operating as Harlequin Reader Service. For a complete summary of the information we collect, how we use this information and to whom it is disclosed, please visit our privacy notice located at https://corporate.harlequin.com/privacy-notice. Notice to California Residents – Under California law, you have specific rights to control and access your data. For more information on these rights and how to exercise them, visit https://corporate.harlequin.com/california-privacy. For additional information for residents of other U.S. states that provide their residents with certain rights with respect to personal data, visit https://corporate.harlequin.com/other-state-residents-privacy-rights/.

HPHM25